PRINCE OF PERSIA
THE SANDS OF TIME

A novel based on the major motion picture
Adapted by James Ponti
Based on the screenplay written by Doug Miro & Carlo Bernard
From a screen story by Jordan Mechner and Boaz Yakin
Executive Producers Mike Stenson, Chad Oman, John August,
Jordan Mechner, Patrick McCormick, Eric McLeod
Produced by Jerry Bruckheimer
Directed by Mike Newell

𝒟ISNEY PRESS
New York

Printed in the United States of America
First Edition
1 3 5 7 9 10 8 6 4 2
J689-1817-1-10060
Library of Congress Catalog Card Number on file.
ISBN 978-1-4231-1780-3
This book is set in 13-Point New Baskerville ITC

Visit www.disneybooks.com

PROLOGUE

There once was a harsh land that few survived and none controlled. Only through bold sword strokes and the sheer force of will did an empire rise from its soil.

That empire was Persia.

By the close of the sixth century, the Persian Empire stretched thousands of miles, from the shores of the Mediterranean Sea to the steppes of China. Its warriors were fierce in battle and its leaders were wise in victory. But the empire was only as strong as its princes, the young men who would grow to become its rulers.

One of those young men was Sharaman. The

crown prince of Persia, he was in line to inherit the throne from his father and become king.

Sharaman knew his destiny and was thus determined to develop the skills that would make him a great king. He was tutored by Persia's greatest scholars and trained by its most courageous soldiers. He cleansed his soul with reflection and prayer in the High Temple and honed his bravery by hunting in the unprotected desert that lay outside the walls of the royal city, Nasaf. He knew that these things would help him. What he did *not* know, what he could not foresee, was how one particular day would change the path of so many lives. . . .

On that particular day, Sharaman silently stalked a desert buck. His attention was so focused on the buck he didn't notice a lioness stalking him. By the time Sharaman heard her deadly growl, it was too late.

The lioness leaped through the air to attack Sharaman. He would have been killed if it had not been for the courage of his younger brother, Nizam, who jumped between them and killed the animal with his spear.

It was indeed a selfless act. If he had not saved his brother, Nizam would have taken his place as crown prince. One day *he* would have become king of all the empire.

Instead Sharaman fulfilled his birthright and assumed the throne, while Nizam became his most trusted advisor. Forever united by the bond of that moment, the young king and his brother fought side by side to spread their empire.

As the king's fortunes grew, so did his family. He had two sons, Tus and Garsiv, who gave him much joy. But his family was not yet complete. . . .

CHAPTER ONE

The foul stench of rotting garbage filled the air. It came from a sprawling garbage heap on the edge of Nasaf. This was home to the waste of an entire city. It was also where poor, homeless children scavenged for leftover scraps of food.

One of those children was Dastan.

His hazel eyes scanned the piles of trash until he spotted a half-gnawed piece of meat. It was covered with flies but was the closest thing to a meal that Dastan had seen in some time. He scooped it up, and three other boys tried to wrestle it away from him.

They only stopped when they heard a nearby shopkeeper call, "Messenger!"

In an instant, Dastan and the others scrambled off the heap and raced to the shopkeeper. The man was holding a package and would pay one of them to deliver it. He eyed them suspiciously.

"You're the fastest one of these scags, aren't you?" he finally said to Dastan.

Dastan nodded confidently. "That's why you pay first."

If this man wanted the fastest, Dastan was determined to get paid for it.

The shopkeeper stared at him for a moment before he relented. Then he handed Dastan the package—and a coin.

Moments later, Dastan was racing through Nasaf. Actually, he was racing *over* Nasaf. Rather than push his way through the crowded streets, Dastan ran freely across the rooftops, jumping from building to building without fear.

This is what made Dastan so much faster than the others.

He delivered the package to a small shop, where he spied a stack of apples. Unlike the food he scavenged from the dump, these apples were clean and ripe. Tossing the owner of the shop a coin, Dastan grabbed an apple, his mouth watering in anticipation. But before he could take a bite, he heard a commotion outside on the street.

Dastan stepped out into the bright sunlight just as a group of Persian soldiers marched through the marketplace. They were impressive in their gleaming uniforms. This was especially true of their captain, who rode alongside them atop a large stallion.

Nearby, a boy named Yusef was playing with his brother. Unaware of the danger, Yusef ran in front of the captain's horse. The stallion reared up on its back legs and dumped the man onto the muddy street.

When the captain stood up, his once spotless uniform was covered in filth. Enraged, he grabbed Yusef and slapped him across the face. He continued to beat the boy until someone stepped out from the crowd to challenge him.

"Stop!" commanded the voice.

The captain turned and saw . . . Dastan.

A mere boy? Daring to give *him* an order? The captain laughed and started to strike Yusef again.

Acting impulsively, Dastan took his apple and threw it at the man, hitting him right in the head. This time the captain was not amused.

He turned his rage on Dastan. "You filthy piece of street trash!"

"I'm not the one wearing horse manure," Dastan replied.

The crowd laughed, which only made the captain angrier. He charged at Dastan. "Run!" Dastan yelled at Yusef.

Both boys scurried away from the soldiers to the edge of the marketplace. Dastan helped Yusef climb up onto the roof of a shop and they began racing across the rooftops as the soldiers pursued them from the street. They were about to get away when Yusef's foot slipped on a tile.

Just as he was about to plunge down to the street, someone snatched him out of midair.

Yusef looked up to see that Dastan had grabbed him with one hand and was holding on to a rain gutter with the other. They were dangling from the edge of the building.

Summoning all of his strength, Dastan swung Yusef up to safety on the roof. But when he did, the gutter pulled off of the building and Dastan plummeted to the ground.

Dastan scrambled to his feet and started to climb back up, but it was too late. Within seconds, he was surrounded by soldiers. There was no escape.

The captain grabbed Dastan and dragged him kicking and screaming into the center of the market. "Witness how the king punishes those who disrespect his army!" the captain pronounced to the people who had gathered around them.

Two soldiers forced Dastan to his knees and stretched his hand over a gutter.

"In the king's name . . ." the captain said as

he raised his sword to chop off Dastan's hand.

Suddenly, a hush fell over the marketplace. Looking up, the captain saw the reason. King Sharaman had arrived, riding on a beautiful black stallion.

Unknown to the soldiers, the king had witnessed the entire event unfold from the shadows of a nearby alley. Now that he had made his presence known, every head in the marketplace was bowed—except for one. Dastan stood, head held high.

"Don't you fear me?" the king asked, more curious than upset.

Dastan nodded. "I do, sire. But if I'm going to lose my hand, I want to look into the eyes of the man who takes it."

Unlike the captain, who had been angered by Dastan's boldness, the king was impressed. Here was a boy who was both noble and brave, two qualities he admired greatly.

"What is your name?" he asked.

"Dastan, sire," the boy replied.

"And your parents?"

Dastan glanced away, and Sharaman realized he had no parents.

In that moment the king saw in Dastan, a boy with no royal blood, the chance to have a son with no eye on his throne. A son he could always trust. So he adopted Dastan as a member of the royal family, as his third and final son—a true prince of Persia.

CHAPTER TWO

Twelve years later . . .

A blinding sandstorm raged across the desert, its massive swirl blotting out the sun. Although it rumbled like thunder, this was no force of nature. The storm was created by something far more deadly and far more powerful than weather and wind.

Suddenly a column of horsemen burst through the flurry, proudly carrying the red and gold battle standards of King Sharaman. They continued riding until they reached the desert's edge. Behind them the storm slowly began to settle, revealing an endless line of soldiers and supplies that stretched from one end of the horizon to the other.

This was the Persian army.

The dominion of the king, it was commanded by his sons.

It had been twelve years since Dastan had been adopted by Sharaman. As he and his brothers grew into men, they had come to represent very different, but equally important, qualities of the empire.

The thoughtful Tus was the kingdom's brain. As crown prince, he would one day become king. Just as his father had, Tus did all he could to learn to be a wise decision maker. He tried to be deliberate in his reasoning and relied heavily on his uncle Nizam for advice and counsel.

The quick-tempered Garsiv represented the kingdom's muscle. He knew he would one day be called upon to carry out the decisions his brother made as king. He was eager to win glory in battle and always ready to unleash his fury on any threat to the empire.

The spirited Dastan was the empire's heart. He was a prince, but he was also a man of the people. He led a group of soldiers who, like him, had come from the streets. He loved the men in his command, and he loved his brothers. But most of all, Dastan loved King Sharaman, the man who had seen the potential for greatness in him.

Now, after a long march from Nasaf, the army had reached its destination. As soldiers began to set up camp, three men in royal uniforms stood apart, surveying a terrain unlike any they had seen before. From horseback, they looked out at a lush green valley that stretched all the way to mist-covered mountains in the distance.

Tucked into this valley was the magnificent walled city of Alamut.

The leader of the trio was Tus, his golden robes radiant in the setting sunlight. "Even more stunning than I imagined," he said softly. While his words were praising, he wore a look of concern on his face.

"Don't be fooled by beauty," warned his uncle, Nizam. The old man's face was weathered with experience. "It's a city," Nizam reminded him. "Like any other." It was his duty to help the crown prince reach the right choice now.

The third member of the group, Garsiv, adjusted the breastplate of his black armor. When he looked down at Alamut, he didn't see beauty. He only saw possible routes to attack. "Soft countries make soft men," he said coldly. "They stoop to treachery and must pay for it."

"Perhaps," Tus responded, considering it for a moment. "But Father has made clear that Alamut's not to be touched. Some consider it sacred."

Garsiv's face turned sour. "The king spends more time in prayer than battle now," he said. "Perhaps he no longer knows what's best."

"Enough," Nizam scolded. "Your father has won honor enough to fill the desert."

Chastened, Garsiv nodded.

"Since our wise father isn't here, the decision rests on me," Tus reminded them. Decisions weighed heaviest on Tus when reason dictated one thing but his heart another. To attack—or not attack—Alamut was one such decision.

"I'll have one last council with my noble uncle and my two brothers," he declared. It was only then that Tus noticed his youngest brother was not with them. He looked around, and there was no sign of him anywhere. "Where is Dastan?"

In the middle of a makeshift ring, two men fought using the ancient martial art *Pahlavani*. As the two clobbered each other with *Karela* clubs, onlookers cheered and booed in keeping with whom they had bet on to win.

One of the fighters, Roham, had the distinct advantages of size and strength, but the other countered with singular determination. He somehow managed to withstand each blow and remain on his feet. The soldiers let out more cries as the two men exchanged hits. It was only the appearance of a herald calling for Dastan that stopped the fighting. Looking at the herald, the smaller fighter smiled. His penetrating hazel eyes were unmistakable. This was Dastan. The young urchin had grown into a strong and handsome man.

"Your Highness, please," the herald pleaded. "Prince Tus has convened a war council."

Dastan took a deep breath and nodded. It was time for him to be a prince again. Dropping his clubs, he quickly started to put on the uniform of a royal officer. He winced with pain as his trusted lieutenant, Bis, helped him tighten his armor over the fresh bruises.

Bis nodded to the men. "About the bets?" he asked.

Dastan rubbed his throbbing shoulder. "Pay them all," he announced, eliciting a cheer.

"Tell me something, Bis," he whispered as he pushed his tongue along the inside of his mouth. "Have I still got all my teeth?"

Moments later, Dastan entered the war-council tent. "He was fighting with common soldiers again," Garsiv snarled angrily when he saw Dastan.

"Roham is hardly common," Dastan corrected

with a laugh. "He hits like a mule. Not a bad cook, either."

"Allow them to strike you," Garsiv said testily, "and they lose fear of us all."

"That's fine with me," he said defiantly. "*Cowards* lead by fear."

Nizam held up a hand to silence the young men. There was much to be discussed, and they did not have time for the sibling rivalry between Garsiv and Dastan.

"You two are brothers and princes," he reminded them. "Save your fury for Alamut."

This caught Dastan's attention. "*Alamut*?" he asked, surprised. "But the king . . ."

They all knew that King Sharaman had instructed them to leave the city untouched. But the situation had changed. "The king doesn't know this," Tus said, motioning to a man in the corner of the room.

Dastan eyed the man. He had pale blue eyes that were cold and nearly lifeless. Opening two giant trunks, the man revealed a collection of deadly weapons.

"Our finest spy intercepted a caravan leaving Alamut, carrying these to our enemies in Koshkhan," Nizam explained. "Swords of the finest workmanship, steel-tipped arrows."

Tus handed Dastan several rolls of parchment. "A promise of payment from the warlord Kosh to Alamut," he explained. "They're selling weapons to our enemies!"

Garsiv pulled a steel-tipped arrow from the pile of weapons. "Such an arrow slew my horse during the battle in Koshkhan," he exclaimed. "Blood will run in Alamut's streets for this."

"Or too many Persian soldiers will fall from its walls," Dastan warned, looking up from the parchment.

"Words won't stop our enemies once they're armed with Alamutian blades," cautioned Nizam. As he had been trained, he was careful to redirect the conversation while still letting Tus make the decisions.

Tus nodded in agreement. His mind was made up. "We attack at dawn," he announced.

Dastan held his tongue. This was not what

his father would have wanted. If Dastan could not stop the attack, though, maybe there was a way to minimize the bloodshed.

"In that case," Dastan said, deferring to Tus, "I request the honor of first assault."

Garsiv scoffed. "I ride at the head of the Persian army," he reminded them. "Dastan leads a company of street rabble. The honor of first blood should be mine."

As was his habit, Tus fingered his prayer beads while he worked toward a decision. "It's said the princess of Alamut is a beauty beyond compare," Tus said. "We'll march into her palace and see for ourselves. There can be no doubt of your courage, Dastan," he went on formally, "but you're not ready for an operation of this importance. Garsiv's cavalry will lead the way."

Tus and Garsiv smiled in anticipation of the battle, while Nizam silently nodded his approval.

Dastan, however, just clenched his jaw. He had not been able to convince his brothers to spare the city, but perhaps there was another path. . . .

* * *

That night, Dastan led a daring raid into Alamut.

Rather than charge the fortress directly, as Garsiv was planning, Dastan thought a sneak attack would be more effective. Gathering his men around him, he ran through his plan. Once everyone was set, he climbed Alamut's outer wall with lightning-fast precision. His company of "street rabble" followed close behind.

"Remind me why we've disobeyed your brother's orders?" Bis asked when they reached the top of the wall.

"Because Garsiv's head-on attack will be a massacre," Dastan explained.

Bis thought about this for a moment. He knew that Dastan meant what he said. But he also knew of the rivalry between the two brothers.

"You sure that's the only reason?" Bis asked.

Dastan gave Bis a look that clearly said, "no more questions." Then, before Bis could argue, Dastan set the rest of his plan into motion.

Under cover of night, Dastan and his men disabled most of Alamut's walled defenses. By morning's first light, Dastan's company had control of the city gate.

Dastan opened it and waved a signal torch toward the army above. They had been completely unaware of the raid.

From his tent, Tus heard the rush of men racing into battle. Hurrying out, he looked toward Alamut.

"He's gotten in," Tus announced to his captains. "Redeploy to the eastern gate."

The officers hurried off to lead their companies as Garsiv slammed an angry fist against the table. The honor of first blood would not be his. The battle was already under way, and there was nothing he could do to change that.

Following his brother outside, he rode to war.

CHAPTER THREE

For more than a thousand years, the walls that surrounded the city of Alamut had repelled all invaders. But it had never faced a rival as powerful as Persia. From the moment Princess Tamina, the famed beauty who—for the most part—ruled the city, saw the massive army encamped beyond its walls, she knew it was unlikely Alamut could withstand this next attack.

So, while Dastan was leading his secret raid into the city, Tamina was conferring with the Council of Elders in Alamut's High Temple. When word of the raid reached her, she was deep in prayer.

"The Persians have breached the eastern gate!" a soldier exclaimed as he burst into the temple's sanctuary.

The council members were stunned. The princess, though, knew exactly what to do.

"Collapse the passages to the chamber," she calmly instructed the soldier, who ran out of the room to relay her orders.

"Go now, all of you," she told the council members, sending them off to brace for battle.

Soon, the only one left in the room was Asoka. Although he was the strongest, most courageous warrior in all of Alamut, Asoka would not be fighting in the battle. He had a far more important duty to perform. He stood quietly as the princess kneeled down and pressed her forehead to the floor.

As she began reciting a prayer, a tremor rumbled through the temple. Soon, a radiant glow appeared from within the column before her as it opened to reveal a hidden room.

Tamina rose and entered the room. Inside, she wrapped an unseen object in an embroidered cloth. With fear in her eyes, she gave the object to Asoka.

"You know what to do," she told him.

Asoka nodded and repeated the orders that had been assigned to him long before: "Above all else, it must be kept safe."

Asoka raced from the temple into a chaotic city. The fighting raged in every direction, although it was more of a rout than a battle.

Alamut had always relied on the walls that surrounded the city for its defense. But Dastan had rendered those meaningless. With the Persian army now inside the city, its superior numbers made it invincible.

There was no time to waste. Asoka sprinted through tunnels and courtyards and slipped in and out of alleys. He made it to the royal stable and quickly mounted an armored stallion. Safely astride, he ducked into an alleyway and was close to freedom. But something blocked his escape—Prince Dastan.

Quickly, Dastan drew his sword while Asoka drew his scimitar. The sound of metal hitting metal filled the narrow alleyway. As Asoka was still on horseback, he had a distinct advantage. Glancing around, Dastan looked for a way to get the upper hand. Then his eyes narrowed.

With amazing skill and speed, he ran up a portion of the wall and leaped onto Asoka's back, pulling him off the stallion.

They quickly began a death-defying sword fight. They twisted and turned, battling back and forth—the best of Alamut and the best of Persia. The fight was close, but then Dastan wounded Asoka, knocking him to the ground.

The bundle Asoka had been carrying skittered across the ground. The warrior reached for it, but Dastan was quicker.

Picking it up, Dastan unwrapped the cloth to reveal a jeweled dagger. It had a glass handle filled with sand that seemed to glow. He smiled and slid the weapon into his belt as a trophy of his victory and continued toward the palace, leaving Asoka behind.

CHAPTER FOUR

The king's army was in full control of Alamut. And just as Tus had predicted, the three princes now marched together into the palace to confront Princess Tamina.

They found her in the High Temple, her back to them. Despite the chaos around her, the princess remained regal. She chanted a prayer, not acknowledging the sound of footsteps until Garsiv stepped forward, knocking over an incense burner.

"Silly songs and scented smoke will do little for you now," Garsiv growled.

Lightning quick, Tamina turned, a knife

now in her hand. Lunging, she was about to use it on Garsiv when her wrist was caught by Nizam.

"Perhaps there's a bit more to her than that," Nizam warned his nephew.

Tus approached and used the blade of his sword to carefully move the veil that covered her face. She was in fact more beautiful than they had imagined.

"For once the stories are true," Tus said.

Just then Dastan entered, still catching his breath from his battle with the Alamutian warrior. Seeing Tamina, he stopped in his tracks, struck speechless by her beauty.

Nizam, however, had no trouble raising his voice.

"We know you secretly build weapons for enemies of Persia," he accused.

"We have no secret forges here," Tamina replied defiantly. "What weapons we have, you overcame."

"Our spies say differently," snarled Garsiv. "Much pain can be spared if you—"

She cut him off: "All the pain in the world

won't help you find something that doesn't exist."

For a moment, the room was silent.

"Spoken like one wise enough to consider a political solution," Tus finally said, seizing an opportunity. He held his hand out to her. "Join hands with Persia's future king."

"I'll die first," Tamina replied simply.

Embarrassed and enraged, Tus barked back at her, "Yes you will!"

The prince motioned to his bodyguard, who pulled a sword and pressed it against Tamina's neck.

Dastan instinctively made a move to protect her. When he reached for his new weapon, the princess saw the Dagger. With a stab of pain, she realized that Asoka had not been able to get it out of the city.

"Wait," she cried. Tus raised an eyebrow. "Swear to me the people of Alamut will be treated with mercy."

Tus rolled his prayer beads between his fingers while he considered this. Then he smiled and motioned to the guard to remove his sword. This time, when he held out his hand, Tamina took it.

From his spot in the room, Dastan felt an odd pang. The cost of taking Alamut was proving high—in many ways.

Later that day, Dastan and Bis made their way through the temporary camp the Persians had set up in Alamut. War horses stood beside tents that served as places to tend to the wounded. As they walked, soldiers called out praises and slapped Dastan on the back. He smiled, trading jokes and remarks. Suddenly, a voice stopped him. Turning, he saw Tus.

"They're calling you the Lion of Persia," the crown prince said. "You've never excelled at following orders."

Dastan nodded. "Tus, I have some explaining to do."

Tus broke into a big smile. "No," he answered with a laugh as he put his arm around his little brother. "We have some *celebrating* to do."

Dastan smiled, relieved. He had stolen the honor of making the first assault from Garsiv, but he had been forgiven. At least by Tus. He was certain Garsiv would not be so generous.

"There is however, tradition," the crown prince reminded him. "Since you took the honor of first assault, you owe me a gift of homage."

Tus motioned to the jeweled Dagger in Dastan's belt. Shrugging, he went to give it to him, but they were interrupted by their uncle.

"He delivered you the city and its princess," Nizam reminded Tus. "I think that's homage enough."

Tus looked at the Dagger, considering its worth. "I suppose it is," he said graciously.

Dastan flashed his uncle a grateful smile and slid the weapon back into his belt.

"First dispatches just arrived," Nizam informed them. "Wonderful news. Your father has interrupted his prayers at the eastern palace to join us. He'll be here before tomorrow's sun sets."

CHAPTER FIVE

The three princes of Persia stood in the palace courtyard, obediently waiting for their father's arrival. They were certain he would be proud of their capture of Alamut. But when the king rode up on his stallion Aksh, he looked anything but proud.

Sharaman dismounted and stormed past his sons without even speaking.

Tus eyed Garsiv and Dastan. This was not good. Sighing, he followed his father inside.

"Do you *forget* whose army you lead?" Sharaman bellowed, when his eldest son stood before him.

Tus's fingers nervously ran up and down his prayer beads. "I was deliberate in my decision," he explained. "As you've always counseled."

"I don't recall counseling you to disobey my orders!"

Tus bit back a retort. His father wanted him to become a leader but rarely let him actually lead. "Father, you give me little ground to tread," he said.

"You have ground to *tread*," Sharaman replied, "not *trample*!"

"We had indications Alamut was arming our enemies," the crown prince responded.

"You better have more than indications to occupy a holy city with my troops," the king snapped. "This adventure won't sit with our allies! But I suppose you didn't take that into account."

Tus couldn't believe it. He had been so certain his decision to attack was the right one. Now he was beginning to doubt it. He turned to Nizam.

"Don't look to your uncle, boy!" Sharaman admonished his son.

"The decision and its consequences rest with

me," Tus said. Then, knowing it was the only way he would regain his father's trust, he added, "I will oversee the search for the weapons myself. I vow I will not stand before you until I hold proof of Alamut's treachery."

Holding his head high, he turned and strode out of the room.

Once his nephew had left, Nizam walked over to his brother and tried to calm him.

"He's eager to know the weight of the crown he'll one day wear," Nizam said.

"*You* don't know the weight of the crown he'll one day wear," Sharaman reminded him.

Nizam bit his lip so as not to respond. They were brothers, but they would never be equals. First as the crown prince and then as the king, Sharaman was always Nizam's superior. But he had long ago learned to mask such feelings. His role was to serve his brother, and nothing would change that. So Nizam moved on to a new subject.

"I've arranged a banquet in your honor," Nizam said. "Your sons and subjects are anxious to see you."

The king's anger began to fade a little. In its place was the exhaustion that came with such heavy burdens. Perhaps a celebration in his honor would improve his mood.

"I'll be expected to smile at this banquet I suppose?" he asked.

Nizam laughed. "And drink a bit."

Sharaman returned the smile. Then, once again, he grew thoughtful.

"Dastan?" he asked Nizam. "He attacked without permission?"

Nizam smiled. "A bit of inspired insubordination."

Sharaman considered this and nodded as he looked out over Alamut. He could not go back in time and change history. Whether he wanted it or not, this holy city was now part of his empire. And the boy he had plucked from the streets of Nasaf was now being called the Lion of Persia.

At that moment, the Lion was very much enjoying his victory. In a palace courtyard,

Dastan and his men were partaking of their own form of relaxation.

Roham, the big soldier Dastan had been fighting not too long ago, stood against a wall. Dastan stood in front of him, a goblet in his hand.

Dastan eyed the man. Then the wall. He took a swig of his drink and then he raced—right at the wall. Leaping, he ran ON the wall—he took one step . . . then *CRASH!* He fell to the ground while his men burst into laughter.

"The third step is the hardest," he said, smiling.

"I didn't see you get to the second," a teasing voice said.

Looking up, Dastan saw his brother Tus. Dismounting his horse, Tus leaned down and offered a hand.

"We've uncovered signs of tunnels on the eastern edge of the city," Tus told Dastan as the younger one brushed himself off. "I'm on my way there now."

Dastan looked surprised. "You'll miss the banquet?" he asked.

Tus nodded. Garsiv and Dastan could handle the festivities in his absence. But there was one thing he had to take care of first.

"You do have a gift to honor our father with?" Tus asked.

Suddenly Dastan's eyes filled with panic. How could he have forgotten? It was tradition!

Tus laughed. "I knew you'd forget," he said, putting a hand on his brother's shoulder. He signaled a servant who handed Dastan a wrapped package.

"The prayer robe of Alamut's regent, the holiest in the Eastern lands," Tus said. "A gift the king will appreciate. You fought like a champion for me," Tus added. "I'm glad to return the favor."

Tus stopped, his eyes going to somewhere beyond Dastan. He motioned to a walkway behind his brother. Turning, Dastan saw Princess Tamina being escorted by Persian guards and servants.

"A rare jewel, but Father's a hard judge of wives," Tus said softly. "Present her to the king for me tonight, Dastan."

"Of course," Dastan replied, happy to help his brother.

Tus climbed back up on his horse, but leaned down to tell Dastan one more thing.

"My marriage to the princess will assure the loyalty of the people of Alamut," Tus told him. "If Father doesn't approve our union, I want you to end her life with your own hand."

Dastan was surprised at this request. He didn't know what to say.

"Someday I will be king, Dastan," Tus went on. "When I am, I will need to trust you, know you will obey my rule." He looked hard into his brother's eyes. "Can I count on you to do this for me?"

Dastan replied—with the slightest of nods.

Princess Tamina stood in her chamber as Persian servants prepared her for her presentation to the king. One of them scrubbed her feet while another dressed her in the ornate Persian style. In her own palace, Tamina now felt like a stranger.

At that moment, Dastan strode into the chamber. He had cleaned himself up and was now dressed for the banquet, the Dagger still proudly displayed in his belt.

"I'm to present you to the king, Your Highness," he said formally.

"So I'm escorted by Prince Dastan, the Lion of Persia," she scoffed as she strode past him toward the door. "Must feel wonderful winning such acclaim for destroying an innocent city."

He started after her.

"Then again, you are a prince of Persia," she continued. "Senseless and brutal."

"A pleasure to meet you, too, Princess," he replied, catching up to her and matching his steps to hers. "And allow me to offer that if punishing enemies of my king is a crime, it's one I'll gladly repeat."

Tamina shook her head in frustration. "And he's thickheaded as well."

After a few more moments in angry silence,

they reached the door that led to the great hall. Dastan leaned close to her, blocking her path. "Don't make the mistake of thinking you know me, Princess," he bristled.

"Oh," she said, eyeing him. "And what more is there?"

Dastan did not reply. Instead he turned to the massive Roham, who was standing at the door. "Wait here with Her Highness," Dastan instructed him.

Dastan started to walk away, but before he did, he turned back to Tamina.

"If you can manage it, I suggest a hint of humility when you're presented to the king," he told her. "For your own good."

CHAPTER SIX

The banquet held in the king's honor was a glorious affair. There was food and music and spirited dancing. Dastan watched as his father went through the motions, laughing and partaking in the jovial atmosphere.

"You've cooled Father's anger," Dastan told his uncle when Nizam appeared beside him.

Nizam nodded. "One day you'll have the pleasure of being brother to the king," he told him. "So long as you remember your most important duty, you'll do well."

Dastan smiled. "And what's that, Uncle?"

Nizam gestured for a servant to refill

Sharaman's glass. "Making sure his wineglass stays full."

Dastan laughed, but noticed that Nizam did not. In fact, Nizam's voice had a hard edge to it. Before Dastan could think much about it, Sharaman raised his hand to silence the crowd.

"I'm told another of my sons has joined the ranks of great Persian warriors," he announced.

The people applauded as Dastan stepped forward and kneeled before the king.

Sharaman took Dastan by the face. "We missed you, Father," Dastan told him, his voice soft, the moment between just the two of them.

"I was praying for you and your brothers, Dastan," Sharaman replied. "Family—the bond between brothers—is the sword that defends our empire. I pray that sword remains strong."

Dastan cast his eyes downward. His father had clearly heard about him disobeying Tus's order.

"I understand, Father," Dastan said. "I thought my actions would spare our men unnecessary losses."

"A good man would have done as you did," the king responded. "But a great man would have stopped the attack from happening at all. A great man would have stopped what he knew to be wrong no matter who was ordering it.

"What I saw in that square was a boy capable of being more than just good, but of being great," Sharaman went on, referring to the day many years ago when he rescued Dastan. He looked deep into his eyes. "Tell me, Dastan. Was I right to hope for so much?"

"I wish I could tell you, Father," Dastan whispered, the weight of the question heavy on his shoulders.

Sharaman smiled. "One day, in your own way, you will."

He hugged Dastan, and the crowd cheered again. Dastan hugged him back tightly. Then Dastan remembered the present that Tus had given him.

"I have something for you," he said with a smile, handing him the gift. "The prayer robe of Alamut's regent."

The king smiled, too. Opening the present, he held it up for the people to see. Then he pulled the robe on. "What can I grant you in return?" he asked his son.

Dastan nodded to Roham, who escorted Princess Tamina over to the king.

"This is Princess Tamina," Dastan told him. "Tus wishes to make a union with her people through marriage."

Dastan hesitated for a moment, worried about what he might be faced with if the king refused Tus's request.

"It's my deepest wish that this win your approval," Dastan added sincerely.

The king looked at Tamina, her big eyes filled with anger, pride, and sadness. "In all my travels, I've never laid eyes on a more beautiful city, Your Highness."

"You should have seen it before your horde of camel-riding illiterates descended upon it," she replied.

A shocked hush fell over the room, and Dastan shot her a look. This wasn't exactly what he meant when he told her to exhibit humility.

"But thank you for noticing," she added.

If the others were offended, Sharaman was not. He thought she was brave and noble. These were the same qualities he had seen in Dastan years before—which gave him an idea.

"Clearly she will make a fine queen," Sharaman said. "But Tus already has enough wives."

He looked squarely at Dastan. "You might take fewer chances if such a jewel waited in your chambers," he continued. "The princess of Alamut will be your first wife. What do you say, Dastan?"

Dastan was stunned into silence.

Sharaman turned to the nobles. "He plunges into a hundred foes without thought, but before marriage he stands frozen with fear. And there are some who say he is not yet wise?"

The nobles laughed, and so did Sharaman. But in an instant his laughter turned into screams of agony.

"The robe," Sharaman gasped. "It *burns*."

Garsiv rushed to his father and tried to pull the robe off him. But as soon as he touched the fabric, his fingers got so hot he had to let go.

"God help us!" Nizam screamed. "The robe is poisoned!"

Suddenly Garsiv's face filled with fury. "The robe Dastan gave him!" he shouted.

"Father!" Dastan screamed as he ran to him and cradled his head in his hands.

"Dastan," the king pleaded as he looked into his son's eyes. "Why?"

"Father, no!"

It was too late. King Sharaman was dead. Without a moment's hesitation, Garsiv turned to his guards.

"Seize him!" he ordered. "Seize the murderer!"

In moments, the room was filled with the sound of heavy footsteps as the guards raced toward Dastan. But he was too stunned to move. He just looked down at his dead father, his own heart near breaking.

Seeing the danger his leader faced, Bis bravely stepped between him and the guards. He drew his sword.

"Run, my prince!" Bis cried. "Go!"

Still, Dastan did not move. Reaching over, Bis pulled the prince to his feet and shoved him toward the door—just as a spear pierced him through the stomach. Groaning, Bis fell to the floor.

The death of his closest friend finally snapped Dastan into action. Filled with fury, he drew the Alamutian Dagger and began wielding it like a man gone mad. For a brief moment, he seemed to have the upper hand—but then a guard attacked from behind. Luckily, Princess Tamina was there and hit the guard over the head with a vase.

She had witnessed everything from her place in the Great Hall. She could not let Dastan escape—or be killed for that matter—without first getting the Dagger back. If that meant helping him, she would do it.

Stunned by Tamina's actions, Dastan paused.

But only momentarily. He had to get out of there—fast. He scanned the room for an escape route. There were too many people between him and the door. It would have to be the window.

He jumped, and so did Tamina. Both of them fell through the air and landed in the fountain below with a giant *splash*.

"What do you think you're doing?" Dastan asked as they stood up in the fountain. He was stunned she had followed him. Was she that desperate to avoid marriage to Tus?

"You may occupy this city," Tamina told him. "But you don't know its secrets. *I* can get us out of here!"

Dastan didn't want Tamina slowing him down. But she had a point. He looked back up toward the third floor, where Garsiv now loomed in the window. They had no time to argue. He nodded his assent.

They ran through the courtyard and down an alley that led to the stables where Garsiv and his cavalry had put their horses. Quickly, they set all of the horses free—except for one. Aksh, the most famous stallion in all of Persia—once the king's, now Garsiv's—and the fastest.

Within moments, they were galloping through a secret tunnel that ran beneath the city. Dastan looked back to see if they were being followed and was happy that they weren't. But when he turned around again, he was horrified to see that they were charging right at a closed gate.

The prince braced for a collision. But Tamina deftly pulled out his sword, whipped it in a big loop, and struck a hidden lever.

The gate flew open. Dastan let out a little gasp of relief as Aksh burst out of the tunnel. Soon they were racing through the desert night, Alamut fading behind them.

CHAPTER SEVEN

Dastan and Tamina rode across the desert for hours, stopping only when they reached the banks of a stream.

There was no question Garsiv would send out a search party at dawn's first light. But for now, Dastan and Tamina were safe.

They were quiet as they caught their breath and Aksh drank from the river. The moon cast shadows on the rippling water, and the air was refreshingly cool.

Reaching his hand into the stream, Dastan let the water gently roll over his fingers. His eyes were downcast, his thoughts hidden.

"Dastan," Tamina said hesitantly. When he did not reply, she repeated his name.

Finally, he spoke. "This stream is a tributary of the river that runs through Nasaf," he told her. "The water they'll use to wash his body."

Dastan's words were soft and full of pain. Tamina stared at him for a moment. "You mourn the father you murdered?" she asked, confused by his reaction.

Dastan looked up, his eyes angry—and pained. "I did *not* murder my father."

Tamina knew better than to say anything. She could see his words were truthful.

Noticing a wound on her arm, Dastan went through the motions of cleaning it. Anything to get his mind off his sadness. He reached into the horse's saddlebags and pulled out a piece of fabric to use as a bandage.

"It was foolish of you to add my troubles to your own," he told her.

"I saw how you looked at me when that blade was at my throat," she said softly, referring to their first encounter, when Tus had instructed his guard to kill her. "You were ready to risk everything for me. I saw that in your eyes."

Dastan looked up, surprised, then instinctively moved closer. "I swore to my brother I'd take your life, rather than let any other have you."

Tamina looked into his eyes and the mood became almost romantic. She flashed a flirtatious smile.

"A dilemma," she said of their situation. "The obvious solution would be to kiss me, then kill me."

She moved closer still, her lips almost touching his.

"But I have a better solution," she continued. "I kill you, and your problems are solved."

Dastan laughed, but Tamina wasn't joking.

She hadn't been moving closer to kiss him. She had been after the Dagger!

She reached for it, but Dastan was too fast and slapped her hand away, knocking the Dagger to the ground. Undaunted, she drew a sword from Aksh's saddle and started to swing it wildly.

For a soldier as accomplished as Dastan, this was more humorous than threatening. He held Tamina back with one hand and picked up the Dagger with the other.

"Perhaps we can find a third solution," he joked.

Holding the Dagger in his hand, his thumb traced the engraving. Suddenly he pressed down on the jewel in the handle. A bit of the bright white sand inside it poured out.

As the sand fell, the world around Dastan stopped. Light and sound contorted, and then everything suddenly seemed to move backward.

When the movement stopped, Tamina was once again leaning in toward Dastan.

"But I have a better solution," Tamina said—again. "I kill you, and your problems are solved."

She was repeating her actions and words from seconds earlier, but was completely unaware of it.

Just as she had before, she reached for the Dagger and Dastan reflexively knocked her hand away. But, this time, when she drew the sword from Aksh's saddle, he was too confused and distracted. He didn't reach out and stop her, and she slashed him across the stomach.

He fell to the ground, grasping his stomach. "Give back what you stole, Persian defiler!" she demanded, pointing at the Dagger with her sword.

He looked down at it. Was it possible . . . ?

"No!" Tamina yelled as he pressed the jewel. Once again the sand fell from the handle, and the world around him reversed.

The wounds in his stomach magically disappeared. When the last grains of sand fell from the handle, the action restarted.

"But I have a better solution—" she said for the third time. Now, though, Dastan knew what to expect and interrupted her.

"Go for that sword again and I'll break your arm!"

"Again?" Tamina asked, confused. Then she looked down and saw that the Dagger's handle was empty. Her eyes grew wide.

"You've used up all the sand!" she exclaimed.

Dastan looked at the Dagger's empty handle.

He pushed the jewel again. This time nothing happened.

"What *is* this?" he asked.

Tamina didn't answer.

"Incredible," he said, piecing it together. "Releasing the sand turns back time, and only the holder of the Dagger is aware of what happened."

He looked at her to see if her reaction confirmed he was right. "He can go back, alter events, change time—and no one knows but him."

As he said this, Dastan began to think about all of its possibilities.

"How much can it unwind?" he demanded. "Answer me, Princess."

"You destroyed my city," she said angrily. Was he pompous enough to think she would just hand over information?

Dastan shook his head. "We had intelligence you were arming our enemies."

Tamina scoffed. "You had the lies of a Persian spy."

Dastan thought about this for a moment. The only proof they had was what the spy had told them. No one else had seen the caravan he'd intercepted. And Tus and his soldiers hadn't found any weapons forges in the city yet.

"Our invasion wasn't about weapons forges," he said, as much a question as a statement. "It was about this Dagger."

"Clever prince," Tamina said bitingly.

"After the battle, Tus asked for this Dagger as tribute," Dastan went on, ignoring the Princess's sarcasm. "I didn't think anything of it. But it was him. *He* gave me the gift that killed our father. He stands to be crowned king. With this Dagger, he could change course at a critical moment of a battle. He'd be invincible." Dastan stopped, as if the next words were stuck in his throat. "Tus is behind it all."

Far away, in the newly seized palace of Alamut, Tus paced. He was no longer the crown prince of Persia. He now wore the robes of the king.

He had written a decree which had been copied onto a hundred scrolls. These scrolls were attached to royal messenger falcons to be carried to the far reaches of the empire. The message was to be read and posted in every market, temple, and village square. It said:

My Loyal Subjects,

I share your heartbreak over the death of our beloved king. That it came at Prince Dastan's hand only makes our pain worse. As such, I have doubled the reward for his capture. My treacherous brother must be brought to justice.

King Sharaman will soon be laid to rest in a manner befitting his glory. I invite all our subjects to mourn his passing. But rest assured our empire remains stable, in the hands of a strong leader.

A new reign has begun.

* * *

As the falcons filled the night sky, the new king turned to his bodyguard and gave him one instruction.

"Arrest Dastan's men," he ordered. "Put them where they'll never see the light of day."

CHAPTER EIGHT

That night, Dastan and Tamina made camp along the bank of the stream. Dastan was too distraught to sleep for more than a few fitful minutes. Instead, he kept reliving the horrible events from Alamut. His father was dead, and everyone thought he was responsible. Yet his own brother had killed his father and was now intent on killing him. His world was collapsing. But by sunrise he had devised a plan.

Tus had to be stopped. To do that, Dastan needed help.

He needed his uncle Nizam.

When Tamina woke, she found Dastan

shredding a blanket and wrapping the fabric around Aksh's hooves.

"What are you doing?" Tamina asked.

"Garsiv can't be far behind us," he explained. "Aksh is the most famous horse in the empire. This will obscure his tracks."

"Tracks where?" Tamina asked. "Where are you going?"

"The holy city of Avrat, where Persian kings are buried," he replied. "My uncle Nizam will be there for my father's funeral. He's the only one I can trust. He'll listen to me, see I was set up by Tus."

Sliding the Dagger into his belt, he climbed up onto the back of the stallion. The pain and frustration of the previous night had now turned into anger and determination.

"You're wanted for the king's murder," she said, stepping in front of the horse. Despite the bad night of sleep and the previous day's events, she still looked every bit the beautiful—and stubborn—princess. "And you're going to march into his funeral alongside *thousands of Persian soldiers?*"

"Step aside, Princess!"

No longer a street urchin, Dastan is now a prince of Persia.

The might of the Persian Empire can be
seen in its vast army.

Garsiv, Dastan, and Tus await their father's arrival
to celebrate victory over Alamut.

Nizam will stop at nothing to be the sole ruler of Persia.

King Sharaman has been poisoned! Garsiv and Nizam are determined to find the killer.

Dastan and Princess Tamina try to flee from the royal city of Alamut as the Persian army hunts them down.

Beautiful and elegant, Princess Tamina is also cunning.

Dastan and Tamina take refuge in an oasis. There, the
princess reveals the power of the Dagger.

Sheikh Amar, with the help of Seso, rules
over the Valley of the Slaves.

Dastan battles a Hassansin as Princess Tamina
flees for cover!

It is time to return the Dagger to its rightful place.
But what will be the cost?

Is it Dastan's destiny to become a great man?
Only time will tell.

Tamina stood her ground. "Every road to Avrat will be covered with Persian troops."

Dastan smiled. "I'm not taking roads," he replied. "I'm going through the Valley of the Slaves."

Tamina's eyes grew wide. Was he joking? The Valley of the Slaves was rumored to be a terrifying place. Parents threatened their children with trips to the valley if they misbehaved.

"You'll never even make it to Avrat," she said, crossing her arms across her chest. "Your whole plan is suicide!"

Dastan looked down at her, his eyes burning with determination. "My brother murdered my father and framed me for the crime," he said. "If I die trying to set that right, so be it."

Tamina knew there was no reasoning with him. Her concern, however, was not Dastan's safety. Nor was it the search for justice. Her concern was the Dagger that was still tucked into his belt. She had failed to retrieve it the night before. She wasn't going to quit until she got it back.

Whether Dastan liked it or not, Tamina was going with him.

The Valley of the Slaves was as desolate a landscape as existed on earth. A molten red sun blazed above an endless sea of sand as hot as fire.

Despite the harsh conditions, some humans managed to survive and travel across it. Many were former slaves and criminals who had come to hide from the people who would imprison them. Most, though, were Bedouins, a nomadic tribe who roamed across the barren terrain managing to carve out a meager existence.

Alone in the middle of the desert, two Bedouins made the slow and arduous journey across the valley. Or at least, two people who were dressed like Bedouins. They were in fact Dastan and Tamina. In an effort to disguise themselves, they had traded clothes with an elderly nomadic couple.

Even in this remote area, they could not

afford to be seen wearing the gleaming armor and robes of royalty. They would be in grave danger if they were spied by any thieves who might suspect they carried valuables. And they would be in *more* danger if they were spotted by anyone aware of the reward being offered for Dastan's capture.

"I don't mind the coarse fabric and clumsy needlework," Tamina complained as she tried to get comfortable in the clothes she had gotten from the woman. "I do mind the unmistakable scent of camel urine."

Dastan couldn't help but snicker. He was leading Aksh by the reins and stopped long enough to get a whiff of her as she passed by.

"I think it suits you," he offered with a smile. Tamina did not return it.

They continued to walk a while, each lost in their own thoughts.

Dastan looked down at the Dagger with its empty handle and then looked out at the desert sand that seemed to go forever. Would ordinary desert sand do the trick? he wondered.

He kneeled over and grabbed a handful of sand which he poured into the handle. Maybe he could turn back time and make this whole awful mess disappear.

"Without the right sand," Tamina assured him, "it's just another knife."

He figured she was bluffing and ignored her. Dastan took a deep breath, pressed the button, and waited.

Nothing happened . . . except that Tamina started laughing at him.

"This sand," he demanded. "You have more of it?"

"Of course not," she replied.

Dastan studied her carefully. "How can I get some?"

"Try standing on your head and holding your breath," she offered with a sly smile.

He realized it was pointless to argue with her. Instead of pressing her for information, he remained quiet and they continued to walk in silence.

The desert trek was difficult for both, but

harder on Tamina. Dastan was no Bedouin, but he was used to desert living. Tamina, though, had lived her entire life in the lush Alamut Valley.

"I'm thirsty," she protested after they'd been traveling a while.

Dastan rolled his eyes and tossed her their lone canteen. She grudgingly accepted it with thanks.

As they continued walking, Tamina tried to figure out what was going on in Dastan's head. She wanted to get the Dagger back. To do so she needed to fully understand Dastan's thinking.

"If you can't show your uncle how the Dagger works," she asked eventually, "why in the world would he believe you?"

"That's not your problem," Dastan replied, giving her little to go on.

Again, silence descended. This time, it was broken when Tamina said, "You know, you really walk like one. Head held high, chest out, long, stomping strides." She imitated him. "The walk of a self-satisfied Persian prince."

Dastan did not respond.

"No doubt it comes from being told the world is yours since birth—and actually believing it."

Dastan had finally heard enough.

"I wasn't born in a palace like you," he said, whirling to face her. "I was born in the slums of Nasaf. I lived if I fought and clawed for it."

He let this sink in. "Then how—?" Tamina asked, stunned.

"The king rode into the market one day and found me, took me in, gave me a life, a family, a home," he answered. "So what you're looking at is the walk of a man who just lost everything!"

Tamina was speechless. There was more to this prince it would seem, than she first realized. Sharaman must have seen something special in Datsan to pluck him from the street.

Not much was said again until they came upon a group of skeletons mounted on stakes.

"Who were these people?" Tamina asked, her voice tinged with fear.

Dastan motioned across the expanse of desert before them. "Years ago, this valley held the biggest salt mine in the empire. Until its slaves rose up and killed their masters."

Tamina nodded slowly, her face turning pale. These skeletons must have been the masters.

"I heard they boiled them alive," he added. "Welcome to the Valley of the Slaves, Your Highness."

The sight of the skeletons silenced Tamina for a while. She tried to keep up but started to fall behind his steady pace.

"I'm desperate for a drop of water," she gasped.

"Well, that's more than we have, since you emptied our canteen hours ago," he answered without bothering to turn around and face her.

He waited for one of her typical responses, but she was quiet.

"A miracle," he said mockingly. "I've silenced the princess."

But she was too quiet. Turning around, he saw that she had collapsed.

"Tamina!" he called out as he rushed to her. Rolling her over, he saw that she was unconscious.

"Tamina! Can you hear me?" He tried to shake her awake.

He reached to get a blanket to help prop up her head. When Dastan's back was turned, Tamina's eyes opened. She smiled.

This was just what she wanted to happen. Taking advantage of the opportunity, she whacked him across the back of the head with a large bone that she had slyly picked up and hidden in her cloak.

Dastan reached behind and felt the bump on his head. A look of bewilderment came over his face. Then, a split second later, his eyes rolled back and he passed out facedown in the sand.

"Yes, Dastan," Tamina said mockingly, "I can hear you."

With Dastan unconscious, she reached down and pulled the Dagger from his belt and stuck it into her own. She quickly hopped up on Aksh's back and spurred the stallion into action.

Dastan had no idea how long he had lain in

the sand beneath the sweltering sun. All he knew was that when he finally began to regain consciousness, he was not alone.

First he glimpsed a shadow pass over him, then another. He squinted as he looked up into the light and tried to make out the figures standing above him.

Although the bump on the back of his head continued to throb with pain, his vision began to return. When it finally came into focus, he wished it hadn't.

A dozen men on horseback surrounded him. They wore a mixture of Persian finery, Bedouin cloaks, and other styles. Each carried an assortment of weapons, and not one betrayed the slightest hint of compassion for the poor soul abandoned in the desert.

Dastan knew immediately—these must be the bloodthirsty slaves that gave the valley its name.

Dastan tried to scramble up onto his feet but was stopped when something landed on the ground between his legs with a mighty *thwack*.

He looked at the object, a tri-bladed throwing knife with African markings.

He gulped.

"Do you know where you are, Persian?" a voice demanded.

Dastan looked up at the speaker. This was the leader, a man named Sheikh Amar, whose face was as craggy and wind-ravaged as the land he controlled.

Dastan nodded.

"And yet you enter still?" Amar said, shaking his head with disapproval.

Dastan remained silent, but nodded again.

"In the heart of Sudan, there's a tribe of warriors called Ngbaka," Amar said, his voice dark, "striking fear into all they cross. Ngbaka are masters of the throwing knife."

Amar motioned to one of his riders, an African who wore a bandolier of tri-bladed knives across his chest. They looked just like the one currently on the ground between Dastan's legs. The rider had another blade in his hand, ready to throw.

"This is Seso of the Ngbaka," Amar went on. "I had the good fortune of saving his life, which means he's enduringly indebted to me. So tell me, Persian who enters our valley uninvited, is there any reason I shouldn't ask him to put his next throw just a bit higher?"

Dastan looked up at the man and smiled. In fact, he did have a reason. One he thought the sheikh would be very interested in hearing. . . .

CHAPTER NINE

Unaware of Dastan's meeting, Tamina rode Aksh through a narrow canyon of rock and sand. She checked the position of the sun in the sky to make sure she was still heading in the right direction. The Guardian Temple was hidden in the mountains to the north. Nobody else knew of its existence, so the Dagger would be safe there.

She stopped for a moment to give Aksh a rest, and when she did she pulled the Dagger from her belt. The handle was now empty, but around her neck she wore a small amulet filled with more of the glowing sand. Dastan had been right to doubt her.

She went to pour the sand into the handle. But before she could fill it, a group of cloaked riders appeared from all sides, trapping her. It was Sheikh Amar and his men.

She quickly slid the amulet back out of view and looked for an escape route. There was none.

Sheikh Amar approached on his horse and looked her over. He smiled and nodded to another rider. Lowering his hood, the man revealed his face. It was Dastan.

"You're right," Amar told the prince. "She's not bad. Could smell better, but we have a deal."

Dastan smiled as he pulled up next to her and took the Dagger from her belt.

"Clever princess," he said bitingly.

Dastan had traded her—as if she were a camel!

With Tamina in their grasp, the group rode out of the canyon and across the desert to the site of an abandoned salt mine. They entered it through a tunnel.

"Such a noble prince," Tamina hissed as they walked. "Eagerly leaping to assist the fallen beauty."

Dastan looked her up and down. "Who said you were a beauty?" he asked.

Seething, Tamina practically stammered her reply. "There must be some reason you can't take your eyes off me."

Dastan laughed out loud. "I don't trust you," he said simply.

They continued to walk. The walls rumbled disconcertingly, and there was the sound of shouting up ahead. Pulling Tamina aside at an opportune moment, Dastan reached toward her neck. Quick as a wink, he pulled off her amulet. Flipping it open, he saw the glowing sand inside. With a satisfied grin, he filled the Dagger.

"When my uncle sees the power of this Dagger, he'll believe our invasion was a lie. Thank you, Your Highness."

Tamina's hands clenched. Dastan had no

idea what power he was dealing with. And she could not risk telling him. Not yet. "That Dagger is sacred," she said instead, trying to keep her voice down. "It's only allowed to leave Alamut if the city falls. Dastan, if the Dagger falls into the wrong hands—"

Raising a hand, he silenced her. "I'll keep your knife safe," he said.

"This is a matter for the gods," she replied. "Not man."

While they were talking, Amar's men had been leading them further and further down the tunnel. The sound of cheering had grown even louder. Suddenly, one of Amar's men grabbed Tamina and dragged her away, kicking and screaming. Dastan was helpless to do anything.

A moment later, sunlight appeared. They had reached the end of the tunnel—the heart of the old mine. Dastan could not believe his eyes. It had been converted into a track where ostriches competed in races and spectators bet on the outcomes, hidden from outside eyes by the walls around the mine.

"Ostrich racing?" Dastan said.

"Every Tuesday and Thursday," Amar replied. "What they lack in beauty, they make up for in fighting spirit. And the races are easy to fix."

After all the terrifying stories Dastan had heard about the Valley of the Slaves, it was simply a home for unregulated gambling?

"Not what you were expecting, Persian?" Amar chuckled.

"I've heard stories," Dastan replied, shaking his head.

"The bloodthirsty slaves that murdered their masters?" Amar offered. "A great story but, alas, untrue."

"What about the skeletons we saw?" asked Dastan.

"Bought from a Gypsy in Bukhara," he explained. "I crafted our lurid reputation to fend off the most insidious evil stalking this forsaken land—taxes."

Amar looked at the crowd. "Of course, there is the small matter of blood feuds," he said, almost as an afterthought. Then, his gaze shifted to the stands surrounding the ring. Dastan followed his look and saw Tamina.

With sudden clarity, Dastan realized what Tamina's role would be here. The stands were filled with young women serving food and drinks to the spectators. Tamina was one of them now, dressed in a rather revealing outfit. Perhaps Dastan had been too hasty in his dealings with the sheikh.

"It's odd, Persian," Amar said, looking thoughtful. "You bear a remarkable likeness to the disgraced prince who fled after murdering the king."

Seeing the glimmer in the man's eyes, Dastan realized that Amar and his men had had their own plan all along. He turned to run, but a knife flew through the air and pinned his cloak against a wooden post.

Dastan looked up to see Seso standing there with a proud smile.

"Have I told you about the Ngbaka?" Amar laughed.

"Yes, you have," Dastan answered.

Amar shook his head. "Your brother Tus has offered a reward for you that, between the two of us, borders on the obscene. I'd turn in my own mother to collect that gold." Amar turned to his men. "Take him to the Persian outpost."

Seso reached over and took the Dagger from Dastan's belt.

"Nice knife," the Ngbaka warrior said before tossing it to Amar. The sheikh looked it over for a moment before handing it to one of his men.

"Melt it down for the jewels," he instructed.

From her place near the holding pen where the ostriches were kept between races, Tamina saw everything. She saw the Dagger get taken from Dastan and watched as it was passed along. This couldn't happen! Suddenly she had an idea. Kicking open the gate, she freed the ostriches, who immediately began to run wild through the crowd.

In the confusion, Dastan broke free and managed to grab the Dagger—and Tamina. Together, they raced across the track, leaving pandemonium behind them as fights erupted and weapons were drawn.

"Get to the tunnel!" Tamina shouted, pointing at the path that led back to the surface.

With Amar and his men in hot pursuit, Dastan and Tamina managed to make it to a gate in the tunnel. Once they ran through it, Tamina pulled a lever, slamming it shut and locking their very unhappy pursuers on the other side. They were safe—for now.

Out of necessity, Dastan and Tamina had once again become partners. They rode Aksh across the Valley of the Slaves until they reached a plateau that overlooked Avrat, the funerary city of the Persian Empire.

From their position on the high ground, they had a full view of the endless line of people winding across the desert floor to enter the city.

"They've all come for my father's funeral," Dastan said sadly.

"There's got to be a hundred Persian

soldiers watching those gates," Tamina pointed out.

She had no choice. She *had* to fill him in—a little. "There's a Guardian Temple hidden in the mountains outside Alamut," she said urgently. "Only the priests know of it. It's the only place the Dagger can rest safely."

Dastan ignored her. His stubbornness was driving her mad. Looking at the emotions running across his face, she knew she had to try to appeal to him once more—and hopefully get through. "Dastan," she said gently, "why do you think your father took you off the street that day?"

Finally, Dastan turned to look at her. "I suppose he felt something for me," he answered.

"It was something far greater than love—the gods have a plan for you—a destiny."

Dastan threw back his head and laughed. "I believe in what I can hold in my fist and see with my eyes," he said.

Tamina sighed. She wasn't getting through to him, and time was running out. "I'm begging you—stop thinking about what you used to be and ask, 'What are you *supposed* to be?'"

Dastan was silent as Tamina's words ran through his head, reminding him of his father and the last words he said to him. Could he become a great man? To figure that out, he needed Nizam. "If you want to stay close to your precious Dagger," Dastan informed her, shaking off his thoughts, "you're going to help me get into Avrat."

She had no choice. Tamina was going to Avrat.

CHAPTER TEN

As dangerous as it had been in the Valley of the Slaves, sneaking through Avrat was even more terrifying. There were soldiers everywhere, and if anyone recognized Dastan or Tamina, they would be captured immediately.

While Tamina cracked nuts and served them to a particularly large dignitary, Dastan daringly wove his way alongside the funeral procession and managed to slip a note underneath the saddle of his uncle's horse. The note directed Nizam to meet Dastan at an out of the way stable near the bazaar entrance. A few hours later, he arrived. Tamina stayed hidden in the shadows, eager to overhear the conversation.

"You should not have asked me here," Nizam said when he saw his nephew appear out of the shadows.

"I had no choice, Uncle," Dastan responded, relieved to see the older man's familiar face. "I didn't kill my father. You know I would never do such a thing."

"Your actions speak otherwise," Nizam replied.

"I had no choice but to flee. It was Tus that gave me the cloak. It was poisoned by his hand."

Nizam listened skeptically as Dastan told him his theory.

"The invasion of Alamut was a lie!" Dastan continued. "Tus is after power. He searches not for forges, but for the sand to fuel a mystical device."

Nizam's eyes narrowed. "This is why you brought me here, Dastan? Mystical devices?" His voice was filled with disdain, but his eyes were oddly excited.

"The *Dagger* is why Tus invaded Alamut,"

Dastan said. Reaching into the sleeve of his cloak, he pulled out a bundle. But, when he opened the bundle, the magical weapon that was supposed to be inside was missing. In its place was a nutcracker.

"Is this some sort of joke?" Nizam demanded.

"I had it, Uncle," Dastan said. "I swear."

"Then where is your so-called evidence?" he asked.

His heart pounding, Dastan turned to confront Tamina. But she was no longer standing lookout. He stifled a groan of rage. She must have taken the Dagger and headed for that Guardian Temple she had been going on about! Then he noticed something about Nizam.

"Your hands, Uncle," he said. "They're burned."

"Yes, from trying to pull the poisoned cloak off your father," Nizam replied.

Dastan thought back to his father's death. Every moment of the terrible scene was seared into his memory. At no point did his uncle try to get the robe off Sharaman. That meant his hands could have only been burned by the poison—*if he had been the one who poisoned the cloak in the first place!*

"Is something wrong, Dastan?" Nizam asked.

Nizam was the traitor. Dastan had revealed the plot to the person who was behind it all. Dastan turned and started to run. As he did, an arrow grazed his side. He looked up to find soldiers everywhere. It was a trap!

Dastan didn't have Tamina's help the way he did in Alamut. But here he didn't need it. Avrat was a royal city of the Persian Empire, one that any prince of Persia knew inside and out.

He quickly made his way to the rooftops, a place he could navigate easily while others could not. Just as when he had been a peasant messenger, Dastan skillfully ran along the roof-tops. Archers fired at him, but with his amazing speed, he not only avoided the arrows but managed to pluck two of them from the air.

Dastan's mind went back to the days when he was a boy living in the streets. Then, he survived by stealing food to eat and stayed one step ahead of trouble by outrunning an earlier generation of soldiers. Now, he just had to do the same.

But one soldier would not give up the chase—Garsiv. Clued in by Nizam, Garsiv had quickly gotten in on the action.

When the brothers met up, anger over disobeyed orders in Alamut and vengeful fury over the murder of their father had Garsiv ready to teach Dastan the ultimate lesson of life and death.

At first, Dastan tried to deflect Garsiv's blows with his sword, but the older prince's ax was too strong and Garsiv was too skilled. Dastan realized he needed to outsmart his brother.

In desperation, he moved over to an ornate wooden stairwell in the courtyard. With each swing, Garsiv's fury grew. In fact, the swings were so hard that they were knocking out chunks of the stairway.

"We're not fighting with sticks anymore, little brother," Garsiv said menacingly.

"I didn't kill our father!" Dastan yelled.

"Then God will pardon you," Garsiv raged, "after your head rolls!"

Garsiv moved for the final blow, but at the last moment, Dastan slid out of the way and the ax dug deep into the wood and stuck.

Unable to free the blade, Garsiv was now trapped and exposed. Dastan grabbed a support beam, pushed off the wall, and spun through the air—landing a powerful kick to the side of Garsiv's head.

Garsiv stumbled to the ground, certain that his brother was about to kill him. But Dastan could do no such thing. He loved his brother and could never hurt him.

Instead, Dastan turned his back on his brother and raced out of the city, his heart breaking with every step. He needed to find Tamina—and the Dagger. He *had* to prove his innocence.

Garsiv angrily paced around the royal dining tent while Nizam ate off an elaborate place setting.

"He won't get out of the city," Garsiv declared.

Nizam took a bite of his dinner before responding. "I'm sure he already has."

Garsiv realized Nizam was right. "I've let you down, Uncle."

"Eat something," Nizam replied, motioning to Garsiv's plate of untouched food.

Garsiv shook his head. "I've been thinking," he continued. "Why would Dastan come to Avrat, where he knows it's dangerous?"

"I've been wondering the same thing," a voice boomed.

They looked up to see Tus entering the tent, resplendent in the robes of the king of Persia.

"I thought you were staying in Alamut," said Garsiv.

Tus winked at his brother. "Changing one's mind is a king's prerogative."

Nizam forced a smile. "A wonderful surprise."

"Tell me about Dastan, Uncle," Tus said.

Nizam shook his head. "I hoped to spare you this." Nizam looked into Tus's eyes and lied. "Dastan hopes to stir a rebellion."

"He wants the throne?" Tus asked, surprised.

"I fear so, my lord," Nizam replied. "This is difficult to say. But putting Dastan on trial would only give him a stage. My advice would be to avoid a trial."

This seemed odd to Garsiv, and he shot his brother a look. Tus nodded. He had noticed it, too.

"Your advice is always welcome to us, Uncle," Tus answered. "But whatever Dastan's crimes, a public trial will best communicate the king I hope to be. Strong, but honoring the rule of law. We are not savages."

Nizam was quiet for a moment and then smiled. "You grow more a king every day," he declared.

"Not without your wisdom, Uncle," Tus responded. Then he turned to his brother. "Dastan must be found. He must be brought to justice."

Garsiv nodded. He would not allow Dastan to escape him again.

CHAPTER ELEVEN

Dastan's search for Tamina and the Dagger turned out to be much easier than he expected. In the middle of the desert, he came across a cluster of camel tracks left by Bedouin nomads. The fact that there were tracks was not uncommon, as Bedouins often traveled the desert in caravans. What caught Dastan's attention were the tracks of one particular camel in the group.

Unlike the others, which all followed straight lines, this set veered wildly back and forth. One of the riders apparently had no experience riding a camel.

He followed the tracks throughout the night, and by early morning they had led him to what had recently been a camp. There he found a single person asleep on the ground.

Tamina. Just as he expected.

"Where did the tribesmen go?" she asked, panicking when she awoke.

"Bedouins set out early," he said with a smile. "Especially if they're trying to ditch someone. Judging from your tracks, you were slowing them down."

Tamina closed her eyes and took a deep breath.

"I had no choice but to leave," Tamina said. "I take it your uncle didn't listen to you."

Dastan shook his head. "Worse than that. While we spoke, I saw his hand had been burned. He said it happened trying to pull free the cloak that killed my father." Dastan took a deep breath. "My uncle made no move to touch that cloak."

"So the burns?" Tamina asked.

"He handled the cloak before then," Dastan

reasoned. "He must have been the one who poisoned it. It wasn't Tus. *It was Nizam.*"

Dastan looked out over the dunes, his face lined with pain.

"I'm sorry, Dastan," Tamina finally said.

"I thought he loved my father. But he didn't," Dastan said softly. "He hated spending his life as brother to the king. He wanted the crown for himself."

Still, Dastan could not figure out how killing Sharaman helped Nizam. Tus was next in line for the throne, not Nizam. Nizam would still not be king. What purpose did all this violence serve, then? He looked at the princess. "What aren't you telling me?" he asked.

She didn't answer. Instead, she pointed behind Dastan. A sandstorm was coming. Using her distraction to his advantage, Dastan snatched the Dagger back from her. "If you want it back, tell me everything. No more lies."

Tamina's eyes darted from the Dagger to the storm and then back again. She had no choice. She nodded.

Quickly, Dastan pulled Aksh to the ground and used the saddle blanket and his sword to make a temporary tent to shield them.

As they sat huddled together, Dastan turned to Tamina. "I know Nizam needs the Dagger," he said. "He's got our army searching Alamut for more of the sand. But what else? What secret lies under your city?"

Tamina looked deeply into Dastan's eyes and decided she needed to trust him. Some force continued to bring them together—perhaps he was destined to help her.

"In Alamut rests the beating heart of all life on earth," she began softly. "The Sandglass of the Gods."

She paused, collecting her thoughts. This was a story that had never been shared with an outsider before. For a moment, the only noise was that of the wind howling outside their make-shift tent. Then Tamina told Dastan the story that had shaped her destiny.

"Long ago, the gods looked down at man and saw nothing but greed and treachery. So they sent a great sandstorm to destroy all, wipe clean the face of the earth. But one young girl survived.

"The gods looked down on her and, seeing the purity within, were reminded of man's potential for good. So they returned man to earth and swept the sands into the Sandglass."

Aksh whinnied, afraid of the storm outside. Dastan and Tamina both reached up and rubbed his stomach. Dastan waited patiently for her to go on, realizing how much this meant to Tamina . . . and possibly to him.

"The glass embodies our existence," she continued. "As long as the sand runs through it, time moves forward and man's survival is assured. The Sandglass controls time itself—reminds us that we are mortal."

"What about the Dagger?" Dastan asked.

"Given to the girl whose goodness won man his reprieve. The blade is the only thing that can pierce the glass and remove the Sands of Time. But the handle only holds one minute."

Her words echoed through the small

space. "If one were to place the Dagger in the Sandglass and press the jewel button at the same time?" Dastan hedged.

Tamina's eyes opened wide. This was her greatest fear. "Sand would flow through, endlessly," she said.

"You could turn back time as far as you like?" Dastan thought back to his father's favorite story. "When my father was a boy, Nizam saved his life while hunting," he told her. "My uncle means to go back in time and undo what he did—*not* save my father. That would make him king for a lifetime."

Outside, the storm was quieting. But inside the tent, Dastan's own storm was only growing.

"The sands contained within the Sandglass are volatile," Tamina warned. "That's why it's sealed. Opening the Dagger while it's in the chamber breaks the seal. The Sands of Time would no longer be contained, and *all* mankind would pay for Nizam's lust for power."

Dastan considered this as the storm finally died down. Shaking the sand off the tent, they stepped outside into the sunlight.

"The secret Guardian Temple outside Alamut is a sanctuary," Tamina told him. "The Dagger must be delivered back to the safety of this sacred home. Give me back the Dagger so I can take it there."

Dastan shook his head. "I'm sorry, Princess. I can't do that," he told her.

Her mouth dropped open at his next words: "I'm coming with you."

"You're going to help me?" Tamina asked.

Dastan smiled as he climbed up onto Aksh's saddle. He reached down and offered his hand.

"We can sit here and chat, or you can get on the horse," he said. He was no longer worried about using the Dagger to prove his own innocence. He just wanted to make sure Nizam never got hold of it.

Smiling, Tamina took his hand.

Tus and Garsiv were determined to capture Dastan and put him on trial. This worried Nizam.

It was not part of his plan. To ensure that did not happen, he needed to enlist . . . help. To do that he travelled to the city of Bukhara, where he kept a sprawling private estate.

As he entered the large marble hallway of his mansion, he was greeted by the head servant.

"I need to speak to our guests," Nizam informed him.

"About them, my lord," the servant answered, trying to remain tactful. "Their practices are unusual. The servants have seen things, heard strange sounds. Last week, one of the horses vanished."

The servant obviously expected this news to have more of an impact on Nizam. But the man only smiled.

"Just make sure the servants keep their mouths shut," he informed him. "Or, I promise you, they will vanish as well."

Moments later, Nizam was carrying a torch as he descended a giant stone staircase to a place deep below the estate. At the bottom of the stairway, he reached an ancient wooden door with the image of a griffin carved into it.

Opening the door, he entered a dark chamber filled with dense smoke that made it impossible to see the walls. The floor was carved lattice, and through it Nizam could see glimpses of a second chamber below, where a mysterious ritual was taking place by firelight.

A figure stepped out from the darkness and smoke and stared at Nizam with deathly pale blue eyes. It was the "spy" from the war council who had helped Nizam convince Tus to attack Alamut. But, here in this haze, he didn't seem to be a spy at all. He barely seemed human.

"I have another task for you Hassansin," said Nizam. "But you'll have to be quick. Your prey has a head start."

The servants had a right to be fearful. The Hassansins were an evil sect of killers that had been banished from the kingdom by Sharaman. They were numb to reality and lived in an almost sleeplike trance. They derived great pleasure from practicing their deadly arts. Yet despite their outlaw status, Nizam had been protecting them for occasions such as this—unbeknownst to his brother or nephews.

"It doesn't interfere with your skill?" Nizam asked, referring to the dizzying smoke that filled the chamber.

"In the smoke we see visions of our future, visions of death," he informed Nizam. "In the trance we can find anything, including your nephew."

Nizam smiled before saying, "Then I hope you will see more death soon."

CHAPTER TWELVE

Far from Bukhara, Tamina's eyes widened in delight. After riding hard for what felt like forever, it seemed she and Dastan might have a break. Up ahead, she spied an oasis of lush green plants and sparkling blue water.

"Our journey is blessed," she said with weary satisfaction. "We'll stop for water and push for the mountain pass by nightfall," she instructed Dastan.

"I think you're enjoying telling me what to do a little too much," he said with a laugh.

Surprisingly, the joint task had brought the two closer. As they traveled toward the Guardian

Temple, they had become a team, working together. Dastan had been impressed by Tamina's ability to withstand and adapt to such an unforgiving journey. And she was taken by the obvious goodness in his heart and the strength of his character.

Now she ably led Aksh to the water, and Dastan began filling their canteens. The oasis seemed almost too good to be true, a thriving island in the middle of a lifeless sea of sand.

Much to their surprise, they were not alone. Also drinking from the oasis was an animal that seemed misplaced in the middle of the desert— an ostrich.

Dastan stared at it for a moment before realizing this meant trouble. The oasis *was* too good to be true. Spinning around to get his sword, he came face-to-face with Sheikh Amar.

The sheikh flashed a devilishly crooked smile as his men emerged from the brush.

"We parted under rushed circumstances," he said with mocking sincerity. "I never got to say good-bye."

Dastan and Tamina shared a nervous look as Amar's men surrounded them.

"We've been tracking you for days," he said proudly. "The little riot you started kept going for two days. Bathsheba here is all that's left of my gaming empire!" He motioned to the ostrich. "So, it occurred to me, the only way to recoup my losses was to track down the young lovers who cast this dark cloud upon me. I need the price on your heads."

Despite the dark undertone to the sheikh's words, Dastan was not listening. He was looking at the dunes near the oasis. There seemed to be sand funnels swirling atop them. This was not good.

"Sheikh Amar," Dastan pleaded, "listen to me."

"I'd rather not," Amar said.

He signaled some of his men, and they grabbed Dastan and started to tie him up.

"Noble sheikh," Tamina implored, "we are on a sacred journey."

Amar laughed. "What's more sacred than Persian gold?"

He signaled once more and some other men began to tie her up as well.

Seso, the Ngbaka knife-thrower, walked up to Dastan and pulled the Dagger from his belt.

"Nice knife," he said with a hearty laugh.

Dastan strained against the ropes that bound him, but there was nothing he could do. He and Tamina were prisoners—again.

Amar and his men had ridden through the desert for days, tracking Dastan and Tamina. They were exhausted. He decided that they would make camp in the oasis and enjoy its comforts before heading off the next morning to turn them in to Persian officials.

But that night, while everyone slept, a group of hooded riders raced across the desert toward them. There were seven in all, riding with amazing precision.

The Hassansins.

When they reached a bluff overlooking the

oasis, they finally came to a stop. Silently they dismounted their horses.

The pale blue eyes of the lead Hassansin looked down on his target. Only two of Amar's men were standing guard while the others slept around a campfire.

This will be easy, thought the Hassansin.

He lowered his arms toward the ground, and there was a flash of green as something crawled from each sleeve and burrowed into the sand. Pit vipers.

Amar's two guards were trying not to fall asleep as they scanned the horizon looking for any potential threats. Suddenly one of the guards flinched and then collapsed onto the ground.

Before the other guard could even begin to figure out what was happening, he spied something moving beneath the surface of the sand.

He stepped back in horror. Just as he was about to scream, a pit viper launched out of the ground like an arrow, sinking its fangs into his neck.

The dead man collapsed in a heap next to his partner, and the snake slid across his body. It disappeared under the sand again as it went in search of its next victim.

The vipers raced toward where the others slept. One moved right past Aksh, causing him to whinny.

The sound of the horse woke Seso. He was fully alert in an instant, ready to attack any intruder. Scanning the area, he didn't see anyone.

Then he noticed the furrow racing through the sand toward him. As he watched in horror, a pit viper emerged from the sand, looking for a target. The viper set its sights on him. Then it flicked its forked tongue in the air and began to coil.

Just as it went to strike, the snake was smashed by a smoldering log and knocked away into the darkness.

Dastan had just saved Seso's life! Even with his hands tied, the prince had managed to grab a log from the fire and use it on the snake.

"Give me the Dagger!" Dastan urgently demanded.

Seso didn't know what to do. He looked over at Dastan's tied-up hands. Then he saw the undulating ground.

"If you want to live," Dastan pleaded, "give me the Dagger."

Seso didn't argue. He used the Dagger to cut the ropes that bound Dastan's hands and passed it to him just as three vipers launched from the sand directly at Dastan. When they were in the air, he hit the jeweled button on the Dagger's handle and everything froze. One viper was only inches from his face, its jaws open wide.

Dastan instantly made note of the vipers' locations as time reversed. Then, with just a tiny bit of sand left in the handle, he let go of the button. He had only managed to set time back for a bit. But that made all the difference.

Now, when the vipers shot into the air, Dastan knew exactly where they'd appear.

With blinding speed, he killed each of the

three vipers with the Dagger. Then he threw it through the air and sliced the fourth and final viper in half just as it was about to strike the sleeping Princess Tamina.

The sound of the battle awoke the rest of the camp. Eyeing the dead and dying vipers, their eyes grew wide—except for Tamina's. Hers narrowed. She knew exactly how Dastan had killed the deadly snakes.

"Persian," Amar said with amazement, "how did you do that?"

Dastan didn't even reply. He looked up toward the bluff and saw the silhouettes of the Hassansins watching them. If they remained in the oasis, it would not take long for them to attack again. There would be no more miracles. The Dagger's handle was virtually empty.

"We have to get out of here," Dastan said as he cut Tamina free. "Let's go! Hurry!"

"It's safe to stop now, Persian," Sheikh Amar said after they had been riding for quite a

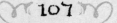

while. They had reached the borderlands and were traveling along a rocky path.

Dastan shook his head. "They won't stop," he assured them. "They track and they kill. That's what they do."

Amar was confused. "What *who* does?" he demanded.

"Those vipers were"—Dastan searched for the right word—"*controlled* by a dark secret of the empire: Hassansins.

"For years they were the covert-killing force of Persian kings," Dastan continued. "But my father ordered them disbanded."

"This sort of secret government killing activity is exactly why I don't pay taxes," Sheikh Amar told Seso.

"They came from the south, where Nizam holds estates," Dastan explained. "He must have disobeyed my father's order. They are no ordinary soldiers, but a cult of killers trained in ancient methods of *Janna.* They'll do Nizam's bidding. Without question."

No one spoke for a moment as they

considered the danger they now faced.

"We can't stop," Dastan said.

"Perhaps you can't," replied Amar. "But we can."

"We could use your help getting to the temple," Dastan told him. Along the way, Tamina and Dastan had given them a brief overview of their mission.

The sheikh laughed at this request. "By crossing the Hindu Kush with a storm building?" Amar replied. "Not only do you draw trouble like flies to a rotten mango, you're also insane."

Amar signaled his men, and they turned to ride in the opposite direction.

"There's gold at the temple," Tamina blurted out.

This caught Amar's attention. He stopped momentarily.

"More than ten horses can carry," she assured him. "Yours after you help us. Tax free."

Sheikh Amar shrugged. Who was he to say no to a good business proposition?

* * *

Dastan, the sheikh, and his men followed Tamina as she led them from the desert up into the mountains. They crossed through the snow-covered Khyber Pass into lands beyond the empire.

Despite the harrowing journey, Tamina showed no sign of suffering. She seemed at peace. Dastan found this far more impressive than her beauty.

Finally, after days of cold, they had reached a more temperate climate. Tamina led them off the path and down into a mist-covered valley. It was in this valley that she would return the Dagger to the stone that it had come from.

Dastan's eyes were wide. From a hundred yards away, the valley had been impossible to see. Yet, here it was, a beautiful place with a few simple farm houses made of stone.

"I was expecting golden statues and waterfalls," Sheikh Amar said disappointedly.

While they rode, Dastan had been thinking

of Tamina and the stories she had told him. Looking at her now, as she gazed at the valley below, everything fell into place. "You're descended from her, aren't you?" he asked. "The girl who 'won man his reprieve.'"

Tamina nodded. "Her descendants are Guardians. It's a sacred obligation, passed down through generations."

She looked at the young, handsome prince beside her. There was a reason he had been brought into her life. She knew it. The Dagger was as much a part of his calling as hers. She smiled, and Dastan returned it. They were in this together.

They continued down into the valley. But when they reached the first farmhouse, they sensed that something was wrong. The village seemed abandoned.

"It's quiet," Dastan said.

Behind the first house, they discovered the reason. Four of the priests who protected the temple were dead, their bodies slumped against the back of the house.

"They have been dead a long time," Seso said, examining the bodies. "Tortured first."

Tamina began to tremble with fear.

"These wounds aren't from normal weapons," Dastan said to Seso.

"Hassansins?" the Ngbaka warrior asked.

Dastan nodded. "They were here," he said quietly. "Nizam knows."

Just then, Sheikh Amar came up to them after surveying the other houses. "All dead," he informed them. "The entire village."

"Tamina," Dastan said, "if Nizam knows this place, we have to get out of here."

Before they could even move, they heard a noise. It was the sound of horses charging.

An enemy was approaching.

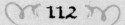

CHAPTER THIRTEEN

The sound of men charging on horseback filled the valley. Dastan grabbed Tamina, but before they could even make a move toward Aksh, they were surrounded by Persian cavalry—led by Garsiv.

Within moments, Dastan, Tamina, and all of Sheikh Amar's men were lined up side by side, guarded by soldiers who had their crossbows poised and ready to shoot.

Garsiv dismounted his horse and strode directly toward Dastan.

"Give me your sword," he said furiously.

"Listen to me," Dastan pleaded.

Garsiv didn't want to hear any of it. "Give me your weapon!" he commanded as he reached for his own sword. "Or do you forsake even that honor?"

Dastan looked into the eyes of his older brother. "There are four dead priests over there," he said, motioning to the bodies. "Murdered by Hassansins on Nizam's order. He's the traitor."

Garsiv laughed and drew his sword out of its scabbard. He pressed its blade up against Dastan's throat.

"Hassansins no longer exist," Garsiv said with a snarl. "You always thought you were so clever."

"This is no trick," Dastan said. "Nizam wants me dead. Wants me silenced. A trial is too public."

Garsiv thought back to the meeting he had with Nizam and Tus. Their uncle had stressed that there should be no trial. He *insisted* that Dastan should not be brought back alive. As Garsiv remembered this, there was a slight flicker in his eye and he eased the pressure of the blade just slightly.

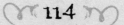

Dastan read his brother's reaction. "He said as much, didn't he?"

Garsiv didn't answer.

"I know it's never been easy between us," Dastan told him. "But still, you and I are brothers."

"Touching words"—Garsiv sneered—"with my sword at your throat."

"Before he died, our father told me 'the bond between brothers is the sword that defends our empire.' He was praying that sword remained strong."

Garsiv thought back about everything that had happened since their father had died. "Nizam recommended your death," he said. "Tus disagreed and ordered you brought back alive."

"Don't you see? Nizam's using the Hassansins to make sure that never happens. He's afraid of what I might say. Who I might tell."

Garsiv considered this for a moment and slowly, finally, removed his sword from against Dastan's neck.

"Tell *me*, Dastan," he said, ready to listen to his little brother.

Dastan was relieved. But just as he was about to explain everything, they heard an eerie whistling in the air, then three metal spikes punctured Garsiv's gleaming breastplate.

"Garsiv!" screamed Dastan as he watched his brother fall to his knees.

From the mist rode a new set of men on horseback. Men far more dangerous than the cavalry.

Dastan knew who they were in an instant.

"Hassansins!" he yelled as he drew his sword.

Within moments a battle erupted between the Persian soldiers and the Hassansins. Amar and his men, captives just moments earlier, were now fighting alongside the soldiers who had captured them.

The Hassansins were the embodiment of cruelty. Each was the master of a different method of killing. One lashed the air with bladed whips, while the one who attacked Garsiv had a row of spikes protruding from his armor, making him into a human porcupine.

The Hassansin leader had more of his deadly

pit vipers hidden in the sleeves of his cloak. It was pandemonium. Dastan had one thought. "We have to protect the Dagger!"

He turned to find Tamina, but she was gone.

Amar moved next to him to help fight off the Hassansins. "Find her, Persian."

Dastan frantically looked everywhere. This was NOT the time for the princess to play her stubborn games. Finally, he spied her climbing up onto the roof of one of the stone houses.

He followed her, and when he got to the top he realized a secret passageway was hidden from view in the rocks above the house. This must be the location of the hidden temple.

He knew exactly what she was planning. She had told him as much. She was going to save the Sandglass by returning the Dagger to the gods and offering herself up as a sacrifice.

Tamina was trading her life for the lives of all humanity.

The thought shook Dastan to the core. Now he was no longer concerned with protecting the

Dagger. He just wanted to protect Tamina. Following her into the cave, he saw her standing in a natural pool. She looked determined, resigned to her fate.

"There's another way," Dastan said quietly. "There has to be."

"There isn't," she told him, turning at the sound of his voice.

"Then let me do it," he said, stepping into the water and reaching for the Dagger.

Tamina shook her head. "Only a Guardian can replace the Dagger. One trained to embody man's goodness before the gods," she explained. "This isn't something you can do."

They looked deeply into each other's eyes. Shielded from the raging battle, they could still hear the sounds of steel against steel and the screams of pain echoing through the temple.

"I'm ready for this, Dastan," Tamina said.

Dastan shook his head defiantly. "I'm not."

Suddenly the battle reached them. The whip-blade Hassansin appeared at the temple entrance and instantly went for Tamina and the Dagger.

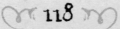

The whip wrapped around her wrist and yanked her against the stone wall, knocking her unconscious.

The next whip was about to cut her in half when Dastan blocked it with his sword. He engaged the Hassansin in a fight to the death.

Dastan had never battled an enemy like this one. The whips came at him from every direction with expert accuracy.

Likewise, the Hassansin had never faced an opponent as skilled and acrobatic as Dastan. They continued to go back and forth, sword against blade, speed versus muscle.

Dastan pushed the fight away from Tamina and the temple and back out onto the roof of the farmhouse. They struggled to maintain their balance as they clashed. Dastan could see the battle still raging below; dead bodies were strewn across the ground.

Just then, Dastan saw an opening and used an acrobatic maneuver to run and push off of the chimney. He flipped into the air and landed behind the killer.

The Hassansin spun and used his leg to knock Dastan off his feet.

Dastan tumbled down the roof and crashed to the ground, the wind knocked out of him.

Before Dastan could catch his breath, the Hassansin leaped down and started to choke him. Dastan frantically tried to break free from the attacker's deadly grip, but the killer just stared down at Dastan with blank eyes that registered no feeling or emotion.

Just as Dastan was sure he was about to take his final breath, the Hassansin's grip suddenly loosened. The warrior fell to the ground.

Gulping for air, Dastan saw that the Hassansin had been killed by a sword which still protruded from his back. Dastan turned to see who had saved him.

Garsiv had managed to summon the strength to climb up on his knees and strike a blow to save the brother he loved.

"Garsiv!" Dastan cried as he reached down and cradled his head. "Hang on!"

"The sword is strong, brother," Garsiv said,

his face pale. "Save the empire."

Dastan knew there was nothing he could do for Garsiv but try and keep him comfortable. He gently laid down his brother's head and then said a silent prayer.

Then he realized how quiet it had become. It shouldn't be quiet. Unless . . . the battle was over, and the Hassansins had disappeared as mysteriously as they had arrived. Dastan's eyes flew open. That could mean only one thing.

He went to check on Tamina, who was standing by the cave entrance, a look of tremendous sadness on her face. "The Dagger?" Dastan asked.

Tamina shook her head. "It's gone."

Dastan looked down at his brother and considered the pain and suffering that his uncle had unleashed. Anger and rage fueled his determination.

He looked back at Tamina and made a solemn promise to her: "We'll get it back."

CHAPTER FOURTEEN

Beneath the faint light of a crescent moon, three cloaked figures rode through the empty streets of Alamut. These were the three remaining Hassansins. They maintained a fast pace until they reached the palace.

The three killers entered through a hidden doorway that led directly to Nizam's chamber. There they found their master sitting at a large wooden table.

"Did you bring that which I seek?" Nizam demanded.

The three sat down, and one of the deadly vipers slithered out from the lead Hassansin's cloak. The snake hissed as it moved across the table, its tongue flickering in the candlelight.

The Hassansin pulled out a gleaming blade, causing Nizam to flinch. With lightning speed the killer grabbed the viper and sliced it open.

The Dagger had been hidden inside the reptile's stomach.

"Dastan lives," the Hassansin warned Nizam.

Nizam considered this for a moment. "In the end, it won't matter," he said. "Time will erase all."

"Death stays with you, my lord," the Hassansin hissed. "As does Prince Dastan. He'll keep coming for the Dagger."

"He won't be in time," Nizam said confidently.

They were on the verge of discovering the Sandglass of the Gods. Once they did, Nizam would have access to the Sands of Time. Then, he would be able to rewrite history.

The next morning, Tus stood on a balcony that looked out over Alamut. He was king, but not without cost. His heart ached for his father and what he thought was the treachery of his brother.

"We've uncovered tunnels beneath the street, my king," Nizam said as he joined his nephew on the balcony.

"Tunnels or not," Tus replied, frustrated, "we've still found no forges."

Nizam gave Tus a knowing nod. "The crown weighs heavily, nephew?"

"More than I ever imagined," Tus replied.

Nizam tried to reassure him. "The forges are here. Be patient."

Tus nodded. "Any word from Garsiv?"

Nizam shook his head. "Not yet, Your Highness," he lied.

Nizam wasn't the only one who knew of secret entrances in and out of Alamut. Tamina had used a secret gateway to enter the city and was now speaking in hushed whispers with her trusted maidservant. Dastan, Amar, and Seso stood a bit off to the side.

"Her friends in the palace say the Persians have broken through the first level of tunnels. They'll reach the Sandglass within hours," she told them when she was done talking to the maid.

Dastan shared a knowing look with Sheikh Amar and Seso. After the battle in the valley, the one-time thieves had fully joined Dastan and Tamina's noble cause.

"Nizam is keeping the Dagger in the High Temple," Tamina added, pointing to the building at the center of Alamut.

The woman spoke some more, and Tamina's reaction caught Dastan's attention.

"What is it?" he asked.

"She says it's guarded by some sort of demon," Tamina translated. "Eyes of coal, skin creased as the desert. Coated in spikes."

Dastan knew exactly who she meant. "The Hassansin."

The woman spoke some more, and Tamina translated for the others: "He casts a curse of death over the sacred chamber. No man can stand within twenty yards of him and live."

Seso spoke up. "Some don't need to stand that close."

The man had a point. Quickly, the four of them concocted a plan. For it to work, the knife-thrower needed to reach the High Temple.

Once Tamina had carefully described the layout of the place, Sheikh Amar and Seso approached the Persian guards at the entrance gate. They did their best to look weak and needy.

"Spare some water?" Amar asked pitifully.

The Persian guard smiled—and then spat on him. The other guards laughed at this. As they did, Amar and Seso pulled shovels out from beneath their cloaks and in a flurry, knocked the guards unconscious.

Just for good measure, Amar leaned over and spat on the guard who had spat on him.

Seso opened the gate to the temple, but before he could go through it, Amar reached up and took him by the shoulder.

"Are you certain of this?" Amar asked him.

Seso nodded toward Dastan. "I owe the boy."

Amar couldn't believe it. "You're an Ngbaka, scourge of the Numidian plane! This nobility business, it's not the cloth that we're cut from."

Seso laughed and put his hand on Amar's shoulder. "My friend, has anyone ever told you that you talk too much?"

They looked at each other for a moment and began to laugh heartily. They had been on many adventures together and knew that there was a good chance this would be their last.

After one final look, Seso ran up the ramp that led to the High Temple. He moved through the halls with stealth and speed until he reached the door outside the sanctuary.

He checked his bandolier. He had only two knives remaining. Taking a deep breath, he burst into the chamber.

There was no sign of the Hassansin. But the Dagger sat atop an ornate pedestal in the middle of the sanctuary.

He stepped toward the pedestal and

suddenly heard the quiet flutter of the Hassansin's deadly spikes flying through the air.

With deft skill, Seso used his tri-blade like a fan to knock the spikes out of the air.

The killer stepped out into the middle of the room, sunlight shimmering off of his deadly spikes.

There were a few columns that offered Seso some protection, but there was no cover near the pedestal. Seso had no choice. He sprinted toward the Dagger, dodging the first flurry of spikes.

Seso flung his final tri-blade—striking true. The Hassansin was defeated. But Seso was injured as well. He could not rejoin the others. So, he did what he could.

He dragged himself up the steps of the sanctuary and retrieved the Dagger. Then, with all of his strength he hurled it through the open window.

It flew through the late afternoon sky and seemed to fall forever until it struck a tree. As always, Seso's throw was right on target.

Standing by the tree, Amar looked up in proud amazement at the Dagger. He pulled the weapon from the trunk and handed it to Dastan.

"Have I told you about the Ngbaka?" he said quietly.

Dastan nodded. "You have."

Sheikh Amar gave a proud smile.

They weren't in the clear yet. This was only the first part of the plan. Now that he had the Dagger, Dastan need to show it to Tus and convince him Nizam was behind everything.

"I hope your brother listens to you, Persian. It will mean both of our necks if he doesn't."

Dastan nodded. He did, too.

Tamina helped sneak him through the palace that had always been her home. Tus was not there when they arrived at his living quarters. So Tamina hid out on the balcony while Dastan waited for his brother's return.

* * *

"Hello brother," Dastan said as Tus entered his royal chamber.

"Dastan," Tus said, surprised.

The king's bodyguards moved to seize Dastan.

"We need to talk," Dastan told him.

"Then talk."

Dastan looked deep into his eyes. "Alone."

Tus fingered his prayer beads for a moment and then turned to his bodyguards. "Wait outside the chamber."

The new king eyed his brother warily and motioned for him to speak.

"Alamut was never supplying weapons to our enemies," Dastan told him. "It was all a lie fabricated by our uncle Nizam."

Tus shook his head. "Nizam? You're mad. What could he gain from such a thing?"

"Beneath the streets of this city is an ancient force," Dastan explained. "A container holding the fabled Sands of Time. Nizam wants to use it to corrupt history—turn back time to make himself king."

"Heresies, Dastan," Tus said.

"I've seen its power with my own eyes," Dastan implored, gripping the Dagger in his hand. "Nizam's discovered its resting place. If we don't stop him, our world could end."

"If you're going to kill me," Tus said. "Best do it now."

Dastan shook his head. "This is no ordinary Dagger," he said. "Press the jewel on its hilt and you will see."

Dastan looked down at the glass handle. There were only a few grains of sand left. He didn't know if it would be enough.

"I should have had the strength to do this before," he went on. "Before we invaded this city."

"What are you talking about?" Tus asked.

He gripped the knife and remembered what his father had told him about great men doing what was right, despite what might happen to them.

"'No matter the consequences,'" he said, quoting his father as he plunged the Dagger into his own heart. He collapsed to his knees, coughing blood as he looked up at his stunned brother.

On the balcony, Princess Tamina stifled a scream.

Nizam rushed into the room, surprised by the scene before him.

"He took his own life," Tus said, bewildered.

"Then God have mercy on the traitor," Nizam said, "for he chose the path of the coward."

Tus looked at his uncle and considered what Dastan had said. He looked down at him and at the Dagger, its jeweled handle sparkling.

"We both know Dastan was many things," Tus said defiantly. "But he was not a coward."

Tus picked up the Dagger. Before Nizam could stop him, he pressed the jewel. Suddenly the world around him froze and began to go backward. Tus watched it all unfold in stunned amazement as Nizam backed out of the room and Dastan's body came back to life.

The final grain of sand fell out right at the moment before Dastan plunged the Dagger into his chest.

"No matter the consequences," Dastan said.

Again he went to plunge the Dagger into his chest, but this time Tus reached over and grabbed his arm, stopping him.

"A moment ago, you died before my eyes," Tus stammered.

Dastan looked down and saw that the handle was empty. They shared a smile of relief and amazement.

"On the day we left for war," Tus told him, "our father told me a true king considers the advice of counsel, but always listens to his heart." He shook his head in disappointment. "I should not have needed such proof from you, my brother. I'm in your debt for reminding me what courage is."

Dastan smiled and reached to embrace Tus. But as before, Nizam burst into the room. He eyed the two warily. "I see Dastan has indeed returned," he said.

Then he looked down and saw the Dagger in Dastan's hands and the fury in Tus's eyes. Without hesitation or warning, Nizam drew his sword and slashed at Tus's body. Dastan screamed as the Dagger slipped out of Tus's hands and slid across the floor.

Dastan dived to get it, but it was picked up by a Hassansin who had followed Nizam into the room.

"Poor Tus, so eager for the crown," Nizam sneered as he took the Dagger from the Hassansin. "And you, Dastan, always charging in, so desperate to prove you're more than something the king scraped off the street. What a glorious mess we are."

"Seems the bond between brothers is no longer the sword that defends our empire," Dastan shot back.

Nizam ignored the young prince. Taking the Dagger, he left the room. The Hassansin stayed behind, ready to kill Dastan.

But Nizam did not know that Tamina was right outside. She stepped into the room just as the Hassansin made a move toward Dastan. "NO!" she screamed, throwing the killer off balance and giving Dastan time to act. Dastan grabbed the Hassansin and made a weapon out of the only thing within his reach—Prince Tus's prayer beads.

Nizam would pay for this . . . of that Dastan was certain.

CHAPTER FIFTEEN

Having escaped the Hassansin, Tamina and Dastan raced to stop Nizam.

"The guardians built passageways underneath the city for secret access to the Sandglass," she told him as she led him down a darkened stairway. She stopped when she reached a carving in the wall. Reaching behind it, she pressed some sort of latch that opened a hidden doorway.

Dastan's eyes opened wide.

"If we move fast enough," she told him, "we can get there before Nizam."

Tamina continued to lead him through a

passageway barely large enough for them to fit through. It was dark, and Dastan could only see a few inches in front of his face.

Suddenly, an earthquake trembled through Alamut.

"The digging is undermining the city," he observed.

Tamina shook her head.

"It's the gods," she replied. "Nizam must have breached the Chamber of the Sandglass. He's almost there."

They continued on. The darkness gave way as they entered a giant chamber with a floor made entirely of golden sand. The sand was perfectly smooth, and in the middle of the room was a golden cupola.

"That will lead us down to the Sandglass chamber," she told him.

Suddenly the ground beneath them shifted, and the floor appeared to drop away. Before he knew it, Dastan was sliding down with the sand, riding it like an ocean wave.

Tamina was able to leap to the golden

cupola. But when she turned to reach for Dastan, it was too late. "Dastan!" she screamed as he disappeared from view.

The sand poured down deeper and deeper beneath the city, until finally Dastan was able to grab hold of an arch that protruded from a ledge. Using all his strength, he pulled himself up and into another underground passage.

For a moment he tried to catch his breath and let his eyes adjust to the darkness. When they did, he looked out over a place the likes of which he had never seen. It was an ancient hidden city. A pit sat in the middle of step pyramids set against the walls.

As he went to make a move he saw something terrifying on the stair before him . . . a pit viper. It lunged at him. With lightning speed, Dastan managed to catch it with the blade of his sword.

His eyes urgently scanned the room for the source of the viper. For a moment, he saw nothing. But then he sensed something behind him and spun around just as the Hassansin leaped down.

The Hassansin wielded two fang-shaped blades in a flurry of speed and steel. Dastan fended them off with his sword. The blades clashed back and forth as they moved across the step pyramids. Any wrong move would send them plummeting into the abyss.

The Hassansin was able to pin Dastan against the steps. Dastan had to drop his sword in order to grab on to the Hassansin's blade and keep it from piercing his throat.

As they struggled, Dastan looked into the killer's cold, dead eyes. They were terrifying.

Then he noticed something even more terrifying . . . a pit viper started to crawl out of the Hassansin's sleeve.

Dastan could do nothing to stop it.

The viper let out a cold evil hiss as its tongue flicked the air. It lunged at Dastan, and the prince closed his eyes, bracing for it to strike.

But it didn't.

When Dastan looked to see what had

happened, he saw that the viper had stopped in midair, inches from his throat.

Turning, Dastan saw Tamina gripping the viper with all her strength. She screamed and shoved the snake's gaping fangs right into the Hassansin's face.

The killer recoiled and stepped back, falling into the abyss.

"Tamina," Dastan said breathlessly, still unable to believe what had just happened.

She didn't say anything. She just grabbed him and pulled him into a deep kiss. But, when the embrace ended, Tamina's knees buckled and Dastan had to catch her to keep her from falling.

Dastan didn't know what was happening. Then he saw two puncture wounds on her wrist.

"The viper!" he gasped.

Tamina nodded. In saving Dastan, she had been bitten. He wanted to try to get her help, but there was no time. She was weakening.

"If the Hassansin was here . . ." she said in a whisper.

Dastan nodded. "So is Nizam."

She pointed down a corridor toward a bright light.

It was a glow with which he was now familiar. It was the glow of the Sands of Time.

CHAPTER SIXTEEN

Carrying Tamina, Dastan followed the corridor until it led him to the massive sandglass chamber.

The Sandglass of the Gods was magnificent. It was colossal and towered above the vaulted room. Its white sand cast an eerie light that danced through the air. As Dastan looked at it, he could see reflections of time shimmering in the glass—brief images from his life.

And then he saw Nizam, equally mesmerized and totally unaware that Dastan was there.

Dastan watched him. On the verge of completing his dark mission, his uncle's face was nearly manical. Just as Nizam held up the Dagger to plunge it into the glass, Dastan stepped out from the shadows with his sword drawn.

"You murdered your own family," Dastan spat out at him.

From the shadows, Tamina looked on. The purity of her spirit was fighting the dark poison of the viper, giving her strength. Her heart ached for Dastan and was filled with horror at Nizam's madness.

Nizam smiled. "At first I thought it would be difficult," he said with a sneer. "But in the end, it wasn't. Just like any war."

"Sharaman was your brother!" Dastan yelled.

"And my curse," his uncle replied. "Do you know what it's like? No matter what lands you conquer, what glory you bring the empire, when you walk into a room all eyes are on the man next to you. And you know, if only on that day so long ago you had simply let him die, it would have been you!"

Dastan screamed and swung his sword at his

uncle, who used the Dagger to fend it off. After a couple of swings, Dastan managed to knock the Dagger free. Then he raised his sword to kill Nizam. "I looked up to you," the prince said with disgust.

Dastan hesitated for just a moment. But it was a moment too long. Nizam pulled out a blade hidden in his cloak and slashed the prince across the stomach.

Dastan collapsed to the floor.

"I never understood why my brother brought trash into his palace," he scoffed. "Enjoy the gutter, Dastan. It's where you'll stay under my reign."

Nizam grabbed the Dagger and plunged it into the Sandglass of the Gods. He pressed the jewel and an endless supply of sand started to pour through the glass handle. Suddenly the world around them began to bend as time went into reverse.

The glass started to crack and seemed certain to shatter.

"Nizam!" screamed Dastan. "Don't use the

Dagger to go into your past. It'll unleash—"

"Unleash what?" Nizam replied. "God's wrath? Hell itself? So what? Better to rule in hell than to grovel upon the face of this cursed earth."

Nizam pushed the Dagger deeper into the glass.

Dastan summoned what little strength he had left, got back onto his feet, trying to wrestle the Dagger away from Nizam. The Sandglass cracked even more.

As they fought, images of the past flashed by. They saw Nizam turning the three princes against each another. Plotting with the Hassansins. Time continued going backward, with images of Sharaman screaming in agony as he put on the poisoned robe.

Nizam flashed a devilish smile at this moment, and the anger Dastan felt gave him added strength. He began to pull even harder. Finally, his strength and goodness won out over Nizam. He was able to pull the Dagger from his hand and out of the Sandglass of the Gods.

When he did, time stopped reversing and the crack began to heal. But the damage was done. The sand that had been released continued to flow, creating a tidal wave. Within moments, Dastan and Nizam were sucked into it and dragged away . . .

EPILOGUE

When the sandstorm cleared, Dastan was no longer beneath the city of Alamut—he was alone on its streets. Nizam was gone. Or at least the Nizam that would remember the events in the chamber was gone.

The sands had stopped flowing, but Dastan had still gone back in time—to the raid on Alamut. He had just fought the warrior Asoka and discovered the Dagger.

Dastan thought back to the hardships and adventures which he had just endured. He had seen the worst of the evil that lived inside men. In Princess Tamina he had seen beauty, strength, and love that he had never imagined. He had come face-to-face with death and survived. And now, those moments had been wiped clear from history.

No one knew that they had happened.

Except Dastan. Despite the difficulty of facing them, these events had not weakened him. They had made him stronger. He was ready to face the future, not as a good man, but as a great one.

He was eager to meet Tamina once again.

He was eager to prove Nizam a traitor and hug his brothers and father.

He was, once again, a prince of Persia.

The sword was strong.

Race back in time to see how Dastan
went from urchin to prince in:

THE
CHRONICLE OF
YOUNG DASTAN

By Catherine Hapka
Based on characters created for the motion picture
Prince of Persia: The Sands of Time
Screenplay written by Doug Miro & Carlo Bernard
From a screen story by Jordan Mechner and Boaz Yakin
Executive Producers Mike Stenson, Chad Oman, John August,
Jordan Mechner, Patrick McCormick, Eric McLeod
Produced by Jerry Bruckheimer
Directed by Mike Newell

Some might claim that the king's palace was
the heart of Nasaf. But to Dastan and the
outcasts he surrounded himself with, a very
different place was the center of their world.
That place was the vast, stinking, fly-ridden
garbage heap that lay just beyond the sprawling
market area. Dastan and his fellow urchins

spent much of their time sifting through this putrid wasteland, the easiest place to find something to eat without relying on charity or theft.

Dastan paused at the edge of a flat rooftop overlooking the trash heap, watching several children squabble over a couple of unripe figs. The eldest couldn't have been more than six or seven years old, and Dastan idly wondered how many years had passed since he had been their ages. It did not matter. On the street, age was not remembered, or minded. Turning, he scanned the other street dwellers crawling over the refuse.

Most of the faces were familiar. There were few on the streets, young or old, unknown to the sharp-eyed Dastan. But his gaze passed over all of them, finally settling on a slim, wiry boy a few years older than him. The boy's dark hair stuck up at all angles from his head; he was dressed in rags with a tattered bit of hemp rope serving as a belt. At the moment, he was helping a wide-eyed little boy dig into a mound of rotting fruit.

The chicken Dastan had captured earlier

had largely given up its fight. Now it suddenly clucked and twitched.

"Keep quiet," Dastan said, tucking the bird behind his back. "I want to surprise Javed."

Dastan whistled, and the wiry boy looked up immediately, his curious brown eyes searching the rooftops. When he spotted Dastan, he waved. He said something to the little boy he had been helping and then hurried over to Dastan. As always, Javed's left arm was tucked inside his clothes. It had been badly damaged in a fire that had killed his family a number of years earlier and was of little use to him now.

"I see you've taken to the rooftops, little brother," Javed called with a grin as he came closer. "Does that mean you've managed to enrage another of our esteemed local shop-keepers with your pillaging?"

"Something like that." Dastan held the chicken behind him. He shifted and squirmed in an attempt to hide it as it twitched and flapped around. "Get up here and you'll find out."

Despite having only one arm, Javed didn't

need any assistance in reaching Dastan up on the rooftop. Backing up a few steps, he ran straight at the building upon which Dastan was perched, and kept running—right up the wall and onto the roof! It was an impressive and handy trick but also a difficult one. Dastan had never quite been able to master it.

"Well?" Javed said. "What did you find?"

"This!" With a flourish, Dastan pulled some onions out of his clothes.

"Ah, not bad." Javed's expression lost none of its cheer as he took one of the onions and examined it then took a bite right through the skin. "And they're neither rotten nor dried out. That's a fine thing. The pickings are slim in the dump this morning."

"And as usual, I see you've given away what little you found to someone else," Dastan said, glancing down toward the young boy, who was gnawing on a mutton bone.

Javed shrugged. "He's new on the streets, having lost his mother just a week ago to a brain fever," he said quietly. "He needed it more than I."

To Dastan, caring too much about anyone or anything was a weakness when one lived on the streets. Javed thought differently. For this reason, it had been difficult for Dastan to trust Javed when he'd first turned up among the homeless urchins. Dastan thought he must have wanted something for his benevolence. Until then Dastan hadn't needed friends, and even now he didn't really want to let anyone else in. Many times he'd thought, if only Javed felt the same way, surely we would eat better.

Still, he knew better than to chide Javed for his softheartedness. It never did any good.

"Oh, I nearly forgot," Dastan said with an air of great carelessness. "I also found this."

He pulled the chicken from behind his back, shaking it a bit to make it squawk. Javed's eyes widened when he saw it.

"Can it be?" he exclaimed. "A whole chicken! Why, King Sharaman himself couldn't ask for more!"

"Indeed." Dastan grinned. "I might even split it with you for a suitable price—say, that worthless old coin hanging around your neck?"

Javed's hand flew to the coin he wore on a thread. "My lucky coin? I wouldn't trade it for all the chickens in the empire!"

Dastan laughed. He knew very well that the battered old coin was priceless to Javed. It was the only thing he had left of his family.

"All right, then." Dastan turned the chicken right-side up and thrust it toward his friend. "I suppose we can share—*if* you are the one to dispatch this creature so that we might eat it."

"Not a chance, little brother!" Javed exclaimed. "You are much more ruthless than I, even at your tender age."

Dastan waved the hen in his friend's face. "Go on," he urged with a grin. "You can do it. Otherwise, I might as well let it go."

"Okay, I'll pluck and prepare it," Javed said, bursting into motion. "But you'll need to catch me first!"

There was a taller building adjacent to the one where they were sitting. Without hesitating, Javed raced over, leaped across, and ran up the wall onto the higher rooftop.

Dastan couldn't resist a challenge. "You'd better find a sharp stone, because here we come!" he shouted back.

Tightening his hold on the chicken's scaly legs, Dastan raced toward the wall that Javed had just conquered. This time he was sure he could do it. He leaped directly at the wall without slowing. His bare feet slapped against the rough stucco. One step up, two . . .

For a second, Dastan thought he was doing it. But then he felt his momentum slow. One foot slipped and then the other. Dastan cried out as he tumbled to the ground, falling onto the chicken.

The alarmed bird let out a squawk and flapped its wings violently. Dastan's grip had been loosened by the fall, and before he knew it he'd lost his hold on the hen's legs.

"Hey!" he said as the bird made a break for it, flapping across a narrow alley to another nearby rooftop. "Get back here, you!"

Dastan stood and brushed himself off, glad

that at least nobody had witnessed his fall. Glancing across the alley, he saw that the chicken had stopped to peck at something. It would be an easy matter to collect her, then catch up to Javed, who was surely several roof-tops away by now. He stepped closer, preparing to make the easy leap across the alley.

"Help!" a terrified voice cried out from somewhere below. "By the names of Zurvan and Ahura, someone please help me!"

Dastan stepped out to the edge of the roof and peered down. A narrow alley lay directly below. It was a dead end, with houses on both sides and a high stone wall at the corner. A man with a patchy gray beard and tattered clothes was pressed up against the wall, looking terrified. Standing in front of him was a couple of nasty-looking youths.

"Don't go far, my tasty friend," Dastan called to the chicken. Then he began to stealthily make his way down into the alley.